LORDAL

LORDAL

STEPHAN AUGUSTINE

The Cavern Press

Los Angeles

This book is a work of fiction. Any references to historical events, real people, or real places are used fictitiously. Other names, characters, places, and events are products of the author's imagination, and any resemblance to actual events or places or persons, living or dead, is entirely coincidental.

Text copyright © 2022 by Stephan A. Hodge

Cover art and design by Jonathan Elliott

All rights reserved. No part of this book may be reproduced, stored in a retrieval system or transmitted in any form or by any means without the prior written permission of the author, except by a reviewer who may quote brief passages in a review. Please do not participate in or encourage piracy of copyrighted materials in violation of the author's rights. Purchase only authorized editions.

Published in the United States by The Cavern Press, LLC.

Visit us on the Web!

thecavernpress.com

The text of this book is set in 12-point Book Antiqua.

First Edition

ISBN 978-1-7358288-1-7

For Jordan

LORDAL

PROLOGUE

ANTHONY

Anthony Monroe...

The voice returned, fading in as softly as a violin and fading out just as beautifully. When it first came, a week ago, I thought it was me. Chatter in my own mind. The beginnings of schizophrenia, maybe.

Anthony Monroe...

It was constant, like someone tapping their foot impatiently in my mind. I couldn't stop it. It wouldn't go away.

Anthony Monroe...

I looked up from the polished floor of the basketball court. Coach Hall was waving his arms frantically, calling out to me. We were in the middle of the state championship playoffs. We were only losing by a few points so it was anyone's game, though at the moment I was sitting on the sidelines trying to figure out what the hell was going on. Coach Hall continued to shout as I stared blankly through him. I couldn't hear what he was saying. I could see his spit flying as he kept going.

Anthony Monroe...

"Monroe!" I finally heard. "We need you on the court! Come on, man!"

I groaned, shaking my head and slapping sense into myself as I got on my feet. My fatigue was greater than I'd anticipated and I fell straight to the floor. I heard the whistle as I pushed myself up and heard "Time out!" shouted. It was the squeaking of shoes on the court that drew me back as I began spinning on the floor.

"Ant? Anthony?" I could hear my teammates calling me but the clearest voice was still the one in my head.

Anthony Monroe...

I gasped as if I was coming up for air when someone grabbed hold of my shoulders. I focused my gaze to see Tyson standing over me. He was looking at me like he was a concerned lifeguard that just saved me from drowning.

"Are you alright, man?" he asked as our teammates looked at me over his shoulder. Dozens of eyes peered down at me, all wondering what was going on.

Anthony Monroe…

I groaned, rubbing my temples as I sat up slowly. I was sweating so much that it began getting into my eyes. The stinging of it is what helped me focus. "It's so hot," I mumbled.

Tyson nodded. He looked over his shoulder and said something to someone. To Coach Hall, I assumed.

"You're going to be alright, man," said Tyson. He held out a hand, helping me to my feet. "Come on, let's get over to the benches."

Tyson helped me sit down and I thanked him quietly. My voice was so soft that I wasn't sure he even heard me. He said something as he left me, but I couldn't quite hear him anymore. There was only one voice again, and it only said one thing.

Anthony Monroe…

"Here." I looked up quickly to see Tyson handing me a water bottle and towel, both of which I took gratefully with my shaking hands. I nodded to him in appreciation and he sat down beside me. I heard the whistle again and the game was back up and running. We watched as our team flew the ball down the court.

"You know what's crazy?" Tyson asked.

"What?"

Anthony Monroe…

I shut my eyes and squeezed the bridge of my nose for a moment, trying to focus. Tyson patted me on the back and laughed. "We might actually win this thing," he said.

* * * * * * *

Anthony Monroe…

We won the game. The team celebrated together in the locker rooms briefly, then scattered to celebrate in their own ways. I was too preoccupied to participate in any of it. I lied to Tyson and told him I would try to meet up later, then I went back to the empty locker rooms and collapsed in the showers. I felt like I was on fire. I hoped cold water would help but it had done nothing to ease my pain. The water turned to steam as soon as it touched me, as if I were actually aflame.

Anthony Monroe…

I stumbled back into the locker rooms, completely unaware of how much time had passed. I was slamming my locker shut again and again, begging for peace in my mind. I had no idea what was happening to me, or why it was happening. That was the real torture.

Anthony Monroe…

I slammed my locker shut, screaming in pain. It felt like my consciousness was beginning to shatter. I was punching my fist into my locker now, over and over with my eyes closed.

Anthony Monroe...

My own thoughts no longer felt like they were mine. I could feel it as I continued to slam my fist into the locker — a blinding rage, like a roaring flame. This had to end.

Anthony Monroe...

I slammed my fist into the locker again. I couldn't hold on much longer. I was losing my mind.

Anthony Monroe...

Had I done something wrong? Did I do something to deserve this? I smashed my head against the locker as I began to feel nauseous.

Anthony Monroe...

Warmth trickled down from my clenched fist. My blood was dripping onto the floor.

Anthony Monroe...

I looked over my hand, observing my bleeding knuckles. It was mesmerizing enough to distract me for a moment, until—

Anthony Monroe...

My eyes shot open as I woke with a start. I had collapsed in my hysteria. I pushed myself up, slipping first in a small pool of my own blood.

Anthony Monroe...

I screamed in frustration, falling to my knees in agony while I held my head in my hands. I rocked back and forth on the floor, flinching as the voice returned.

Anthony Monroe...

I could feel it. There was a burning presence in my mind whenever I heard the voice. It felt like I was losing control, or maybe my sanity. My vision was blurring. I was blacking out.

Anthony Monroe...

I cried out in pain as I fell back to the floor. My thoughts and memories were no longer mine. They were replaced by memories of other lives—and deaths. Deaths I had never experienced were now mine. The pain was mine. It was as if my very soul was bleeding.

Anthony Monroe...

There had to be a reason this was happening to me. I sat up again and held my head in my hands, desperate for just a moment of peace.

"Anthony—"

"Please!" I shouted, shutting my eyes. "Just tell me what you want!"

Anthony Monroe...

"Ant?" said Tyson, crouched beside me. He was holding one hand out to help me stand and put the other gently on my shoulder. He looked at the blood on the floor, my face covered in snot and tears, and decided not to mention it. "Come on, man. Let's get you home."

I shook my head. I could feel vile thoughts and memories flooding my mind again. The flames burning my flesh. Death creeped into my thoughts—hundreds of deaths—like a montage of pain and suffering.

Anthony Monroe…

"Ant," said Tyson. I had forgotten he was with me. "Ant," he said again. "Your nose."

I put my hand up slowly and pulled it away. Fresh blood ran down my fingers. My vision blurred red. The pain was immense now. I struggled to my feet. I couldn't see, punching out wildly to steady myself against something. My fist connected with the locker, punching the door in slightly. I screamed as a searing pain shot through my body. My mind imploded. The world around me sank away, flipping on itself as it continued to cave in on itself.

Anthony Monroe.

There it was, back in full force now. In frustration, pain, or perhaps pure desperation, I punched my fist into the locker again. The door crumpled under the force. My hand ran through what felt like wet, warm liquid. Beads of sweat ran down my neck and face as I pulled my fist free, before repeating the act again.

Anthony Monroe.

It began to feel like flames were licking at my fist as I pounded the locker over and over again. It was the only thing holding me to this world — to reality. I was still in the locker room. This was all just in my head.

Something broke inside me as I hit the locker again and again. I'm not sure what it was. Maybe it was my will. Maybe it was my faith. Maybe I lost hope. I was slowly slipping away from the world to the rhythm of my punching. I surrendered.

The world blinked out of existence before my eyes. My breath escaped me. I was no longer in the locker room but in some strange, twisted twilight dimension.

The sky above cleared and became my window to reality. I peered up to see Tyson bloodied and beaten. His chest was caved in as if something had gone through him. His face was nearly unrecognizable, save for his eyes. They stared lifelessly down at me, betrayed. I watched as a hand reached for Tyson's body. The hand, which I realized was my own, plunged into his chest. My hand skirted inside his chest cavity. After a few seconds, my arm began to tug at the still heart of my best friend. I heard the squelching of muscle and the scratching of bones shifting as they snapped. My hands raised the heart in the air. After a moment of study, they began to peel off layer after layer of muscle until it was deemed ready to be eaten. The window became sky again as I could only assume I began to eat Tyson's heart.

I fell to my knees. There was nowhere to go. I was trapped in my own mind.

I think we're going to be good friends, boy.

"Why are you doing this? What are you?"

Your mind is no longer your own.

Your soul is mine.

STEPHAN AUGUSTINE

Your vessel is mine.

Feel my flames as they course through your veins.

Anthony Monroe, you are now the host of Lordal.

SECTION 1

THE REBIRTH

ANTHONY

LORDAL'S APPETITE WASN'T SATED BY TYSON'S heart alone. He returned my body to me in an alley near Santa Monica Pier, standing over the remains of a young woman. She'd been torn apart, just like Tyson, with her chest ripped open and her heart gone. There was blood everywhere, slowly trailing out of the alleyway, running down the walls of the building we were behind, pooling around the woman's remains. I quickly realized that I was covered head to toe in blood, some fresh and some from Tyson. Maybe there had been others as well. I had no way of knowing for sure.

I began to vomit where I stood, avoiding the corpse of the woman as I did. I watched as her blood flowed towards my vomit and mixed with her blood, a disgusting mess that only made me puke again. I was lightheaded, fatigued. I needed to rest, take time to gather my bearings. I had no idea what was happening to me but it had left me tired and drained.

The sound of sirens nearby brought me back, snapping me out of my dizziness for a moment. I needed to figure out what was going on, before something else happened that wasn't within my control. Somehow, through it all, I knew for certain that I would never see my family and friends again. I would never finish college. I would never have the chance to play in the NBA. My life was over, replaced by the horror of having a bloodthirsty demon possessing my body and mind.

I'm not bloodthirsty.

And it seemed I would never have another private thought. It was impossible to explain but I could feel Lordal inside me. His strength, his mind, his fiery wrath. It was all waiting to be unleashed on the world. I truly had no control. Yet, strangely, part of me wasn't afraid. I understood that I could do things, things that ordinary people couldn't, but I wasn't a superhero or a demigod. This power flowing through me, the awakening of this ancient demon, wasn't a gift or a blessing. It wasn't some miracle bestowed upon me by a loving Creator. This power was a curse — a burden — and I was already suffering.

I felt a newfound confidence and bravado that must have come from the demon, because I still felt my human sense of urgency and panic. People would be searching for me. Even if they weren't at the moment, I needed to get off the streets. I was a young black man covered in blood, and only one of those things was needed any given day to get me killed by a cop.

I stumbled forward a few steps, my body ready to go before my mind could figure out where it was headed. What was my next move? I couldn't guarantee anyone's safety, so I couldn't ask anyone for help. Lordal could take control at any moment. If I couldn't do anything to save Tyson, I didn't trust that I could do anything to keep anyone safe.

I cried out in frustration, flicking my arms down and spraying blood across the alley. With my options being so bleak I needed to start making some decisions, and fast. I started grasping in the depths of my mind trying to figure out my next steps. I closed my eyes and took deep breaths until I was calm, until I could think rationally.

I needed to change out of these blood-soaked clothes. That was my first priority, and I was familiar with the area. I knew where I could go. Getting up, I took one last look at the woman's body behind me before I set out into the night.

* * * * * * *

WALKING TO THE PROMENADE FELT LIKE A WALK of shame. It was as if I was drunk off my ass. I was blacking out, then finding myself closer to my destination before blacking out again. Every light—from cars, stoplights, streetlights—blinded me, disoriented me. It made me want to vomit every time.

Worthless boy.

"What the fuck are you?" I panicked as I continued stumbling down the street. The voice was still in my head. Part of me had tried to dismiss it as part of my insanity. I didn't know if it was reassuring to know it was real.

I'm a man, you ignorant bastard.

Or rather, I was.

"Yeah?" I asked, looking around as my body began to grow warmer. I wiped my forehead of the beads of sweat running down it. "Well, what the fuck are you now?"

I looked schizophrenic talking to myself. Luckily, that wasn't entirely abnormal in the city. I ducked behind a dumpster then as a squad car rolled by. I didn't know if they were looking for me but I wasn't going to risk it. It was probably best to take off some of my bloody clothes. Luckily, a shirtless man in the city was also not entirely abnormal.

You need to rest.

I was starting to burn up. I wiped the sweat off my forehead again with my shirt before I tossed it into the dumpster.

You're not handling your transformation well.

"My what?" I whispered harshly, peeking around the corner before I continued to the Promenade.

Our merging.
You need to slow down.

"I can't slow down."

My head was buzzing. I could hear the chatter of police radios all around me, then their sirens as they flooded the streets. Someone must have found the woman's remains.

Your body can't handle the stress.

"What?" I mumbled. The buzzing was becoming a pounding headache. It was making me feel sick to my stomach again. "What's going on?"

You need to regain your strength.

"Why do you even care?" I asked, still praying that this was all a horrible nightmare. There was just no way this was real.

I would prefer to have a host for longer this time.

"What do you—" I was dozing off, or maybe blacking out again. I couldn't exactly tell, but I couldn't stop it either way. "What do you mean?"

You're not my first host, Anthony Monroe.

This is my curse. Now it's ours to share.

Till death do us part, and most of the time, not even then.

His words haunted me as I finally lost consciousness.

LORDAL

"Don't move, kid."

I cracked an eye open at the bright light shining in my face. I held up a hand to ward off the beam of the flashlight. Just beyond it stood an officer holding his weapon drawn at his side.

I pointed at it with a finger from my hand in the air and said, "You really want to do that?"

The man seemed hesitant, seemingly aware of the carnage taking place in the city tonight. The blue and red lights flashed across our faces as we stared at each other. I glanced toward the street where his patrol car was sitting.

"Waiting for the cavalry, are we?" I asked, shrugging my head in its direction.

"Shut the hell up, kid!" He held his gun up at me. "You have the right to remain—"

I lunged forward then, forcing his gun into the air as he fired a shot into the wall behind me. I twisted his wrist, forcing him to release his weapon. He crumpled to the ground in front of me, dropping to his knees as I twisted his arm.

"Silent?" I finished his sentence as a flame sprang to life in my free hand and I held it to his face. His eyes widened as he stared at the hellfire in bewilderment. I could see in his face it was something both extraordinary and terrifying to him. It was always the same reaction with mortals.

"Please," he began to beg for his life as I brought the flame closer. "Please don't hurt me."

I released his arm then, extending my other hand toward him. "Keys."

The officer slowly reached down into his pocket, producing the keys to his car. He dropped them softly into my hand and I clenched my fist around them before pocketing them. I flicked the flame out of my hand before kicking the officer in the chest, slamming him into the same wall his missed round was embedded in. He grunted on impact, slumping to the ground with his head hung low, but still alive.

Leave him alone!

"Shut up."

I stepped toward the officer, grabbing him by the head and lifting his face up so I could look him in the eyes. I brought my other hand back up, reigniting my flame.

Don't, Lordal! Please!

The boy seemed to forget what I was. His pleas for a show of mercy would go unanswered, at least from me. Perhaps God was still listening for his prayers, but He had abandoned mine a long time ago.

    I slammed my hand into the officer's face and the flame exploded across it. He immediately began to scream, his face melting with a single touch of my demonic flame. I quickly released my hold on him, tossing him aside as the flames spread across his body. He squirmed on the ground as he attempted to extinguish himself, but it was to no avail. I turned away, ignoring the last of his cries before he became silent.

    I made my way to the patrol car as the flaming remains of the officer turned to ash. I didn't bother looking back, there was no need. The flames of Hell consumed all.

ANTHONY

WHEN I CAME TO, I WAS WALKING ON THE SIDE OF the road, wearing clean clothes, all alone. Redwoods towered over me like the giants they were. I felt safe under them, protected. The patrol car Lordal had stolen was nowhere to be seen and I was already feeling fatigued, as if I'd been walking for days. How long had the demon been in control?

"Where the hell are we?" I asked, though there was no response. I realized the more pressing question seconds later and asked, "How long has it been since Santa Monica?"

I shuddered at the memory of it all. I leaned back against a tree. Thousands of thoughts raced through my mind. Thinking at all hurt my mind now, what with the background chatter of another person present in my thoughts. Lordal's entire existence broke my concept of reality. It would have even if he wasn't a bloodthirsty monster. Sadly, he was.

I am not bloodthirsty.

"How long has it been since Santa Monica?" I asked again while I had his attention.

LORDAL

Santa Monica?

"The officer, Lordal. The woman…" I needed to pause to hold back my tears. "Tyson."

Since our merging?

Two weeks ago, give or take a day.

It is no longer relevant.

"No longer relevant," I repeated, disgusted by his indifference. "You've ruined my life."

Shut up.

You had no life.

"Asshole."

It was as if I could feel my blood boil as Lordal reacted to my defiance, but I knew he wouldn't kill me. If I died, he died.

Can you feel that?

I looked up then. Lordal was right. I did feel something. I thought it was him overwhelming my senses.

Someone is coming.

They were maybe a mile away. It was strange that I could smell that. It was strange that I knew.

"I smelled something, but—" I got back on my feet, surveying the woods around me for movement. "I thought it was animal shit or something. Let's start moving again."

You need to learn to use my abilities.

They've been following us for three days.

"You were the one in control."

There is still so much you do not understand.

Here, I will show you.

Lordal's abilities suddenly flooded my mind, becoming a part of my own understanding: demonic stamina, durability, heightened senses, strength; I could be the ultimate superhuman. The only downside being that if I lost control, I was unleashing a bloodthirsty demon into the world.

I am not blood—

Wait.

I noticed it too. The scent following us was closer.

"What the hell is that?"

Stay alert.

Someone is closer than you —

Something whistled through the air behind me, piercing into me before I could turn. I screamed as I toppled down to the forest floor. There was suddenly an arrow buried deep in my shoulder. I roared as I snapped it, the pain blinding my senses. Another arrow zipped through the air above me, nicking my ear as I ducked back down.

You left the arrowhead in, boy.

You must remove it.

Now.

"Shut the fuck up, Lordal. I'm dealing with something here."

Another arrow from a different direction buried itself into the tree next to me with a loud thunk. I leapt up and began to search for my aggressors amongst the trees, spinning in circles as I felt myself grow weaker. Everything began to blur and I stumbled into a tree, holding myself up against it.

The arrowhead, you fool.

It's coated with poison.

    I didn't need Lordal to tell me that at this point. Somewhere between hearing his voice and hitting the ground again, another arrow whizzed past, just another blur in my vision as the poison slowed me down. Reality was warping around me. My senses were betraying me as the poison contaminated my bloodstream. My blood suddenly began to boil again; there was a heat that started in my sides, rising up my back to the arrowhead. I gasped as the air grew hot in my lungs and steam began to rise off my skin. It felt like I was on fire but the poison was passing. I reached back and pulled the arrowhead out as Lordal's cursed blood became my own, literally burning the poison out of my veins, curing me of the toxins.

    Just as I began to get back up again, two more arrows slammed into me. One struck me in the lower back, the other in my chest as I spun from the impact of the first. I stumbled backwards and fell into a small trench, snapping the arrows inside me as I rolled to the bottom. I groaned as I felt the poison once more. Reality was beginning to warp around me again as Lordal's blood tried to save me, but there was too much poison this time. I was starting to black out as I struggled to get back on my feet.

It's no use, boy. We must rest.

We won't die but we need time to heal.

Our fate is out of our hands now.

    If the demon was giving up, what could I do?

"So," I heard a voice call down from above. I saw a figure towering over me, far larger than the trees behind it. A monster, I thought, just like me. I was a monster now; it was only right that another monster came along. "This is where you've been hiding," said the monster.

Before I could find some way to defend myself, the monster slid down into the trench and brought a massive boot down across my face. My head lurched back and my eyes slammed shut.

****

Wake up, Anthony.

Wake up!

I lurched to a start, panicked by the voice of the demon. I was alive. Somehow. My vision was blurry. The last thing I remembered was an arrow slamming into me, then hitting the ground. I was too tired to stay awake. My eyes started to close slowly.

Wake up!

I groaned as I forced my eyes open again. I remembered the poisoned arrows, the monster. It was all slowly coming back to me. My senses returned to me just as slowly. When I could feel my body again, I could feel the restraints immediately. When my vision finally cleared, I could see that my arms and legs were chained to a massive redwood. The chains had been pinned to the tree by a massive rod that kept me locked in. Even with Lordal's strength, it would take some effort to free myself.

My head still felt foggy, like a hangover from the depths of Hell. "Lordal, what the fuck?" I said quietly, unsure if my captors were nearby.

Devil's Bane, boy.

There was enough poison in you to kill a cryptid.

We're only alive because the poison has killed me before.

"What do you mean?"

My curse will never allow me die the same way twice.

I doubt there's anything left on this Earth that can kill me.

You're welcome.

Immortal. I was basically immortal, cursed to live the rest of my days with a demon. If Lordal had already died of old age, was I ever going to physically age again? Was I okay with that? Maybe eternity could have some upsides. I struggled to think of anything positive that could come from an endless life and thought of nothing. Outliving loved ones, going mad from the constant state of understanding that that was how it would always end, the mere idea of living through everchanging time periods and knowing none of it would last. That last one could be interesting, though.

LORDAL

Pay attention, you fool.

"Well, well, well…" someone started from behind me. He stood in front of me then — a rugged man with a rough beard, wearing all black. His hair was long and tied up in a messy bun. He had a tattoo just above his collarbone, on his neck. I didn't know the symbol. I did know that the sword hanging from his side was a katana, and I found myself hoping that Lordal had been killed by one before. "Look at who's still alive. You know, I told them I'd find you. The others doubted me, told me I'd die hunting the mighty Lordal. But I don't believe the stories about you. I mean, look at you, tied up like a dog to a tree. Pathetic."

I lunged forward, struggling against my restraints.

He's a demon hunter.

"That's obvious," I whispered harshly. The Hunter didn't seem bothered by the fact that I was speaking to Lordal. Unfazed, even.

His tattoo — it's his clan symbol.

I have never seen it before.

Their swords are ancestral, passed down through —

I lunged forward again and felt myself get yanked backwards, as if a magnet were pulling me to the ground.

Generations…

I looked at my arms and wrists, ignoring Lordal. The chains and cuffs had symbols on them as well. "What the hell are these?" I shouted in frustration, still yanking on the chains.

"Hell iron, strong enough to restrain any demon. Even yours," the man told me, unsheathing his sword. The blade had an unnatural glimmer to it. The redwoods were shading us from the sun, which made its shine all the more mysterious. "This sword is made of holy steel. A gift from the Heavens to slaughter creatures like you. A perfect blend of magic, metal, and the holy language of angels."

We're lucky to be alive.

I chuckled. I didn't feel lucky at all.

I don't recognize his clan.

His holy blade has never struck me down.

The fool can kill us at any point.

I understood. The curse. The blade in the man's hands could kill Lordal — kill me. The Hunter took my head in his hands then and inspected my face. "I must say," he started, "you don't seem all that dangerous."

"Yeah," I said sarcastically. I spit in his face. "Unchain me. I'll show you how fucking dangerous I am. We'll see how long you last."

Nice.

The Hunter shook his head as he wiped my spit off. "We'll see. You won't be so confident for long."

"You're not going to be so cocky when I get out of these fucking chains."

The Hunter laughed, walking back to wherever it was he'd come from behind me. I screamed in frustration, struggling against my restraints.

"Lordal," I whispered. "Do something."

Even I can't overpower the magic of hell iron, boy.

It was only then that I realized how fucked our situation truly was.

* * * * * * *

I SCREAMED IN AGONY AS ELECTRICITY PASSED through me. A demonic roar escaped me as the current ended, releasing my body from its constriction. Sweat ran down my face as my head lowered back down. Watching it fall to the ground was my only distraction. Otherwise, the overwhelming stench of my own burnt flesh was all I was aware of.

"Why are you doing this to me?" I gasped, barely managing to form the words. I could hardly breathe anymore. The simple function had become excruciatingly painful. My tongue felt thick and heavy in my mouth, still numb from the electrical current that had gone through my body. I had never been so dehydrated and I thought to myself how it was true what they said. People in Hell really did want ice water.

The Hunter laughed as he delivered a swift blow to the pike in my chest. Blood dripped from my mouth to the ground. The patch of grass I stood over was already stained crimson from the time I'd spent chained to the tree. My blood had soaked the earth so thoroughly that now it simply pooled at my feet.

"It's my responsibility to humanity to see that you die. You are possessed by great evil, and so it can only be balanced by the prevailing good. It is the greatest honor to destroy you."

He's sadistic.

I nodded my head in agreement, too weak to speak. Too tired to think. The Hunter had rambled on for days about how killing the host of Lordal was some sort of privilege. There was no misunderstanding his intentions. He'd made them clear from the beginning.

He hasn't even tried his holy blade.

He's a fool, or he's enjoying this.

For days now, the Hunter had tried numerous ways to end my life. I could see that he was starting to become frustrated with his failure. Honestly, so was I. At least he was having fun. For me, it was the worst. I was tortured to death, had a moment of rest in a spaceless limbo, then awoke in the woods, restrained to a tree by a psychopath eager to do it all again.

No matter what he did, I returned. Lordal had died many times, apparently, in many ways. Even now, with a massive generator and some jumper cables attached to a rod that was rammed through my legs, and with a pike in my chest, I could still feel my body healing.

"Are you ready for the next buzz?" the Hunter asked, yanking on the cord of the generator. "Because I am."

He yanked the cord a few more times until the generator revved to life, then leaned against it as he admired my death. My body instantly went tight as the current flowed through me. I felt my jaw lock and tasted blood as I bit my tongue in half. The convulsions started and I felt my flesh burn as the electricity scorched me alive. The Hunter remained unfazed, remaining expressionless as the generator shut off. I slumped forward, held up only by the chains restraining me to the tree. I'd lost the strength to stand days ago.

"Nothing to say now, smartass?" said the Hunter with a smile. I wanted to kick his teeth in, make him choke on them. "Come on, kid. Tell me how to end it and it'll end."

"If you want to kill me so bad," I took a second to breathe, "figure it out yourself."

"You're already damned. You're going to Hell. That won't change." He held my head up and looked me in the eyes. "That isn't even my fault. I didn't put the demon in you. Help me get rid of it before it can hurt someone else."

He let go of me and I shook my head slowly, too weak to look up at him. I heard him sigh in annoyance. I listened to his footsteps carry him away, before the sound of him yanking on the generator's cord started again. I braced myself. He didn't say a word, just yanked on the cord again and again until the generator revved up. My head lurched back, not missing a beat as I convulsed from the shock. Blood oozed from my body, running over charred skin as it seeped past the pike in my chest.

Only a few more seconds, I thought. Then I could rest again. I found myself welcoming the moment of peace I would find in death.

* * * * * * *

Do you hear that?

My head rolled to the side as I started in my half-conscious state. My eyes opened slowly. It was nighttime now, though I had no way of knowing if it was even the same day. A quick look around showed that the Hunter was still gone. Apparently even monsters needed sleep.

Listen, boy.

My head was pounding. I didn't hear anything. I just wanted to close my eyes and rest.

Wake up!

"Fucking hell, man," I whispered, irritated. The last thing I wanted was to wake up the Hunter. "What? What do you want?"

Listen.

"I don't—"

Then I heard it. The low hum of an engine, of a vehicle. Two headlight beams bobbed into existence over a hill a mile away before sinking out of view. The sound of the engine was growing louder and louder. The vehicle was getting closer. I was so beaten, so broken, that instead of hope, I assumed it was the Hunter returning.

It isn't.

"How do you know?"

Don't forget what I am, boy.

Trust me.

Right.

Trust the murderous, super-powered demon inside me.

Nothing can go wrong with that.

"What should I do?" I asked as the beams of light reappeared half a mile away.

Scream.

It felt like Lordal and I were finally starting to get on the same page. That's what days of torture did for bonding, I supposed. We needed to get out of these chains, and that was only going to happen if we got help. If there was a chance that this person could hear me, I needed to take it.

"Help! Please, help!" I shouted into the night, praying I was loud enough to be heard. "Please! Help me!"

The vehicle turned my direction and slowly approached. It was a truck. It rolled to a stop alongside the trail just outside of the clearing. I heard the door open, then shut, followed by the crunch of leaves under their weight as whoever it was approached.

I was suddenly and quickly filled with dread. I just shouted at the top of my lungs and the Hunter had to be nearby, so if he hadn't come to shut me up, it must be him coming now. If it wasn't, he'd be here soon. He must have felt so smug hearing me beg for help. I closed my eyes and waited for his snarky comment to come.

"My god," I heard a woman whisper.

I opened my eyes slowly only to be blinded instantly by her flashlight. "Do you mind lowering that a bit?" I asked through squinted eyes.

She lowered it away from my face and I could see her clearly. She was wearing a khaki brown uniform I didn't recognize, maybe a park ranger. She also wore a badge, though I couldn't read it from across the clearing. She rushed over to me, grabbed my head, inspected my eyes, then looked at the chains around my wrists and ankles.

"I'll be right back," she told me as she ran back to her truck. She ran off and my mind drifted back to her badge. Even if she was a cop, I needed her help to get out of this mess. I could run away after. Whatever happened though, I knew I couldn't let her take me to a station or hospital. My thoughts were interrupted by her return. She was speaking into a radio in one hand, carrying bolt cutters in the other.

"We're too deep in the forest for backup," she said as she put her flashlight under her arm. "But don't worry. I'll get you out of here," she continued as she put the bolt cutters to work on my restraints. "Can you tell me your name? Who did this to you?"

I shook my head, too weak to speak. The adrenaline was wearing off. I suddenly remembered how exhausted I was. The officer cut the first cuff off and it fell to the ground. I looked down at my wrist, all cut up from struggling against my restraints. I flinched as I tried to move my fingers, but I powered through the pain and formed a trembling fist.

The hell iron has touched us for days.

The symbols are scarred into our flesh.

We'll heal but we need to get out of here.

The officer put her bolt cutters to the next cuff and grunted as she used all her strength to free me, but she did it. I was free. I collapsed to the ground, rubbing my wrists in disbelief.

Anthony.

Not now.

Anthony!

The gunshot rang out just as I began to feel my strength returning. I ducked instinctively at the sound. The woman hit the ground next to me. Her eyes stared lifeless at me—a fresh bullet hole between them, the back of her head blown out where the bullet had exited.

Should've listened, boy.

The Hunter approached me slowly, holstering his handgun and brandishing a hell iron knife that I recognized from my days of torture. I got to my feet, feeling my blood begin to boil over the death of my innocent savior. The Hunter paused as I took a step towards him.

"Don't move," he barked.

"What're the odds," I said calmly. "You're not so cocky now that I'm out of those fucking chains."

The Hunter chuckled as he unholstered his handgun again. "I just remembered, I liked you better when you were dead and chained to a fucking tree."

Don't fear the gun.

Keep him from drawing his holy blade.

Nodding to the inner dialogue, I took another step forward. This time, the Hunter didn't budge. "Look," I said, pointing at the officer's radio. "Backup is coming."

No, it isn't.

"It won't be long now." I pointed out into the woods, at her truck. "Even if they don't find us, they'll find her truck. Then her body."

Brave, boy.

He's calling your bluff.

Lordal was right. The Hunter ignored me, closing the distance between us in the blink of an eye, causing me to stumble backwards as he brought his knife down to my chest. I scrambled to get back on my feet, then kicked his leg as hard as I could. He cried out as he fell back, while he retrieved his handgun. I took cover behind a tree, only narrowly avoiding a bullet.

"Is that the best you got?" I shouted, peeking out from behind the redwood. The gun fired and I ducked back. A bullet slammed into a tree a few feet away from where I stood. "Alright, show off," I muttered to myself.

Do not let him use his holy blade.

He doesn't have it with him.

Then he wasn't expecting this.

I stepped back out into the clearing, searching for the Hunter. If I could just get past this psycho, we could walk away. With everything happening, I hardly had time to realize I'd begun talking with Lordal within my own thoughts. It was without a doubt clear now that our deaths together had done something to strengthen our connection. Our minds had grown closer to being one.

Behind you.

I turned to the Hunter, who planted his foot on my chest and kicked me down. I hit the ground and scrambled back, putting distance between us as he continued marching forward.

"Get up and face me!" he yelled. He had a crazed look in his eyes.

My natural impulse was to yell back something sarcastic, even now, but the man moved so fast that he was bringing his knife down over me with a blood-chilling scream before I fully understood what was happening. I closed my eyes in fear and put my arms up, trying to defend myself. I didn't care if Lordal had died from a hell iron knife through the skull before. I sure as shit didn't want to find out what it felt like.

The demonic heat reached new levels inside of me just as the Hunter began to overpower me. A massive surge of heat exploded from my outstretched hands and I flinched as the air burst into flames around me. The blast knocked me back, hitting the ground so hard that it knocked the air from my lungs. When I opened my eyes, there were massive flames that threatened to burn the whole forest to the ground. Whatever I had just done saved my life.

I sat up as I caught my breath, one hand supporting my weight and the other holding my cracked ribs. I could already feel Lordal's flame healing them but the discomfort was still there. I looked around my surroundings, trying to piece together what had just happened. There wasn't much left to see. The clearing had been torched to nothing. The ground around me remained dimly lit by a handful of tiny flames dancing around before they flickered away. A circle of ash was formed around me, indicating I was responsible for the fire. Maybe I was.

The officer's body was caught in my blast, reducing her to ashes. All that remained of her was a couple of scorched bones. The heat inside me wavered at the sight. I never even got her name. I closed my eyes, taking a moment to thank her in silence.

Anthony, we need to go.

I was about to head deeper into the forest when a groan from the burnt brush caught my ear. I turned, looking through the wreckage of my torturer's camp. Sprawled out in the dirt was the Hunter. His injuries from the blast were horrid, so grotesque that I had to look away when I caught sight of him. His arms were so scorched that bone was visible under melted flesh. His face had melted in places as well, where it didn't completely burn off. Something suddenly came over me, a rage like I'd never felt before. I grabbed the man and hoisted him up with supernatural strength. I held him by the neck, crushing his tracheae.

"Tell me who sent you." I demanded as I slammed him into the same tree that he had chained me to for days. He began to squirm, reaching out for anything to grab hold of that might help bring me down. I tightened my grip around his neck as he struggled to break my hold. "Tell me!"

He can't speak, boy.

I loosened my grip enough for the man to beg for his life. "Please..." he barely managed to gasp out.

He won't talk.

He's been trained for this.

Just finish him.

I strained against the demon's influence. The man's life was literally in the palm of my hand. His fate depended on my ability to suppress Lordal long enough to stop him from strangling his next victim.

He tortured us for days!

I shook my head as if doing so would shut Lordal up. I looked into the dying man's eyes. The uncertainty in them showed just how much he had underestimated our power. My grip tightened as I remembered how many times I had died at his hands. Over and over again, I suffered. This was my chance to make him feel the pain he had inflicted upon us. He was lucky death would only happen to him once. Lordal's influence was nearly blacking me out. His rage was blinding me.

Lordal, no.

Sweat dripped from my forehead as I struggled for control. I groaned as I felt the heat begin to course down my spine, spreading through my body.

"Lordal, wait. You can't just—"

I do as I please, boy.

I dropped the man to the ground, gasping for air as it felt more and more like I was being burned alive. I even knew what that actually felt like now.

"No. I won't let you have my body," I said as I stumbled back, holding my head in my hands. "We're doing this my way now!"

A demonic roar escaped me, driven by Lordal's rage. I could feel him fighting back against me like nothing I'd ever felt before. It felt like fire washed over me, scorching my entire body. I screamed in agony as the pain flooded my mind.

Stop resisting, boy.

There will be others.

This one will be the example for what's to come.

"STOP!" I shouted, and it suddenly ended. I felt myself collapse as the heat left my body. I felt the cold rush in. "I won't let you do it," I whispered, shivering. "Not anymore."

Lordal's silence echoed in my mind as I gathered myself. I pushed myself up to my feet, struggling as my strength seemed to have disappeared. I stumbled over to the man, looking down at his tarnished figure. My fingers had left dark rings around his neck. He could barely breathe, let alone give me anyone's name. He was a dead man, whether Lordal had his way or not, but at least he saw me for who I was. Not a demon, just a possessed kid — a cursed man. I was not a monster like him.

"Kill me…" he gasped through shallow breaths. "Please… The pain… It all hurts."

He tried reaching out for me as I walked past. I looked down at him one last time. The silence was only betrayed by the crackling of small fires around us, and his labored breathing. This was his perspective, I realized. This was what he saw every time he killed me.

"Goodbye, Hunter." I looked away from the disfigured man. He deserved this fate. He would die suffering, and if someone managed to find him out here, maybe he'd reconsider his line of work. Either way, I wouldn't be the one to end his life. I wouldn't let Lordal corrupt my thoughts with his influence.

I looked around at the remains of the Hunter's camp one last time. There was nothing much left of it, but then I realized two things. The first was that I never learned his name, and I wasn't even sure if he knew mine. The second was that—

We don't need to worry about his holy blade.

"Why not?"

He's dying.

He didn't pass it down.

Without the proper ritual of descent,

the blade will become useless.

"What about his chains and dagger?"

Leave them.

They're harmless without a hunter.

"If you say so," I mumbled, turning away from it all then and walking off into the night.

****

I STARED OUT AT A RIVER WE HAD JUST FOUND, watching fish jump in the stream as the sun rose. There was a campsite across from us, though the campers were still asleep. I had been waiting for maybe thirty minutes now, contemplating what to do. Part of me so badly wanted to rush into some friendly camper's arms and beg them to take me back to Los Angeles, but I knew I couldn't do that. I understood what my life was now.

You should have killed him.

I sighed, looking down at my chest in the early morning light. You would have no idea looking at me of what I had been through. My body had fully healed. I thought Santa Monica was a nightmare but it didn't even compare to my time in the forest.

He was a monster.

More than you or I.

Well, more than you, at least.

I had no idea how old Lordal was, nor did I care to know, but I found myself wondering if he ever found his existence tiresome. I imagined that one cursed to walk this earth forever could become lonely—depressed, even. I stared at my reflection in the river, contemplating how he might feel. The demon himself seemed to have nothing to say, which was interesting. He had made it quite clear that he could hear my every thought, maybe even before I knew what I was thinking.

I watched then as, across the river, birds flew up into the sky. I had to admit, all things considered, that I was doing okay. I wasn't being tortured. My body wasn't being controlled by a bloodthirsty demon.

I'm not bloodthirsty.

Ignoring him, all in all—despite being wet, cold, and hungry—I was doing pretty good. I looked back at the camp as I realized that they must have been how the officer found me. They must have heard my screams. That poor woman was just doing her job and now she was dead, killed for being a good person.

He murdered that woman.

"You murdered my best friend," I said quietly. "You're a fucking monster."

It wasn't intentional, boy.

Every host goes through the bloodlust.

Some are luckier than others.

Blame yourself for being too weak to stop me.

"How dare you!" I caught myself before I had the mind to shout again. I was furious with the demon. I didn't want to speak to him in my mind. I was worried it would somehow make it easier for him to assume control of my body. "Let's get one thing straight. You're a killer, no better than the Hunter. Both of you are monsters."

Of course, you idiot boy.

I do what I must to survive.

That's not what made him a monster.

He was dangerous —

a lost soul that deserved to burn by hellfire.

"Two wrongs don't make a right."

Who cares?

Don't speak to me of right and wrong, boy.

I've been alive a very long time.

He's still dead and I'm not.

I felt a sudden distance between us in my mind. It was a strange sensation. Maybe that was the reason demons needed hosts: to have a moral compass.

I turned to watch the sunrise over the lake downriver. The beauty felt surreal after everything. I imagined what the future would be like then, with Lordal forever trapped inside my head. I could go and find a place like this somewhere far from anyone and anything. I could keep the world safe from Lordal. I could always have moments like this one. There could still be peace for me somewhere on this Earth.

"How curious," said a voice from behind. "You seem unaware of fate itself."

So much for your little daydream.

I spun around in a panic, allowing the heat to pass through me. Fire leapt from my hands and into the trees, bursting into tiny explosions against them. I wasn't going to let myself get captured again, but there was no one to be seen behind me.

Look at the flames.

You'll burn the whole forest down.

Clench your fist and breathe.

The brush had begun to burn from the fires I'd started. I did as I was told and my flames extinguished themselves before they started another forest fire. "You heard that too, right?" I asked, turning back toward the river. "Or am I hearing things?"

"Fortunately for you," said the same voice, "there's only one voice in your head."

There's actually two.

I shouted in surprise, stumbling backwards off the rocks. My jaw dropped as I tried to process what was happening before me. Rising from the lake was the head of what I could only describe as the shadow of a man.

Well, would you look at that?

A phantom figure.

"A what?" I shouted, stopping myself from screaming. I didn't want to startle the sleeping campers. I scrambled backwards into the trees and slammed my back hard into a trunk. A soft groan escaped me as the spots vanished from my eyes.

It's a projection of a person somewhere else in the world.

"What the fuck do I do?"

Calm down, boy.

It isn't corporeal.

"Calm yourself, child," the phantom figure started. Floating before me was a being made of pure darkness, wearing a long phantasmal cloak also made of shadow. "The clock is ticking."

"What the— Who—" I stammered.

Stop talking.

You're embarrassing yourself.

"There's no time," said the phantom, waving its hands quickly. "You're needed elsewhere. I've been sent to fetch you." The phantom rubbed its chin, as if deep in thought. It floated forward, hovering over me as it inspected me, as if something troubled it. "I do have one question, actually." The phantom floated backwards to stand on the rock I had been sitting on.

"What?" I started blurting out questions. "What are you? Who are you? Send me where? What the fuck is happening?"

"Why did you spare that man's life?" the phantom continued, ignoring my downward spiral completely.

"What?" I asked again in the same confused, irritated tone.

"He brutally murdered you for days. He killed that woman. Yet when his life was in your hands, you—" The shadow shook its head, as if realizing its error. "Forgive me. It isn't relevant. I'm simply curious."

I stared at the phantom, still perplexed by its very existence. Then, as I thought about it, I was even more perplexed by the question. Saying it was because I didn't want Lordal to have his way felt childish.

When I didn't answer right away, the phantom nodded its head. "Perhaps you are fit for the burden you carry," it said as it waved its hand in a circular motion toward me.

The wind began to pick up. The cold air whipped at my face. I squinted my eyes as I began to feel myself lifted up above the brush. I felt the energy all around us surge, though I had no idea what was happening.

My concept of reality was once again fundamentally shifted, though this time it felt exciting—not terrifying. This was real magic. It was extraordinary. Then, as I realized I still had no idea what the fuck was going on, I began to panic. I scrambled and flipped onto my feet as the wind continued to lift me up off the ground.

"What are you doing, shadow guy?" I shouted over the hum of power in the air. I dug my feet deep into the ground, drawing strength from the heat inside me. I turned to look back, struggling to see against the wind. Darkness had begun to creep its way from the forest, trailing slowly toward me.

"Abandon your fear," the phantom told me as it began to sink into the ground, merging with the shadows of the trees, "for this is your world now." The shadow figure began to sink back into the ground, merging with the shadows of the trees. Before the figure vanished, I heard its voice one last time. "Be well on your journey, Anthony Monroe."

The wind picked up stronger than before. The shadows began to rise from the ground in waves as they reached my feet. The darkness began to wrap itself around me, slowly forming into a cocoon. I cried out as I was submerged in an endless night. The ground slipped from beneath me then. A sudden weight found its place on my shoulders, forcing me into a downward spiral. The air was freezing, as if I was caught in a snowstorm. The heat inside me intensified, keeping me warm as the world around me grew colder and colder. The weight on my shoulders grew heavier still, sending me further into the dark. I couldn't breathe. I was drowning in the shadows, being suffocated by darkness. Fear filled my mind.

Then, as quickly as it began, it ended.

I felt myself being lifted back into the world. My fear subsided as the shadows began to fade away, as air filled my lungs. The cocoon of darkness began to peel away, layer after layer, until there was nothing but the scene before me.

SECTION 2

THE ORACLE

ANTHONY

THE COCOON EVAPORATED SLOWLY INTO THE cracks of the walls around me. I dropped gently, unaware until then that I was a few feet in the air, stumbling forward as I landed.

Where the hell are we?

"How the fuck would I know?" I mumbled with a certain tone, looking up at the buildings that towered over us much like the redwoods of the forest. We were in an alleyway. The sun was high in the sky and birds flew overhead. The sound of cars and honking horns came from both ends of the alley.

"Oh, thank God! You're finally here," said a voice from behind. I turned to see a blond-haired man, slightly tanned by the scorching sun. He didn't look much older than me, though the stubble on his chin may have aged him up. His eyes were a pale green. His outfit was excessive in this heat: a trench coat with black jeans and black boots. I'd just gotten here and I was already sweating. How he was rocking his outfit in this weather was beyond me. "I was worried you wouldn't show," he continued. "Was Luka's form of travel okay? I haven't gotten to try it yet, myself."

"Who's Luka?" I asked. "And who the hell are you?"

And where are we!

For the love of —

"And where are we?" I added, slightly annoyed.

The man shook his head, chuckling at himself. "Sorry. Where are my manners?" He extended his hand and I hesitantly shook it. "Joseph St. Claire. It's a pleasure to meet you. And you are?"

"You don't know who I am?"

Joseph shook his head. "No, which is..." he began to walk around me, examining me up and down, "incredibly odd, considering my role. I do, however, know of Lordal. You are his host, correct?"

Don't answer that.

"I am," I plainly admitted, unsure how Lordal expected me to lie after everything we'd been through.

Idiot.

Ignoring the demon, I asked Joseph about what he had said before. "You said something about your role? What role?"

"I am the mighty Oracle, seer of all things," he said casually, waving his hand dismissively as he walked out of the alley.

The Oracle? I had just experienced what I could only call magic, and being burdened with Lordal had opened my eyes to the supernatural. I had no reason not to believe Joseph St. Claire other than the fact that I didn't know him, or trust him. He looked back at me then, noticing that I wasn't following. I had been staring after him, dumbfounded.

"Come along, host. This is no place to waste away your immortal life. We have things to get done." Joseph St. Claire didn't wait for my response. He shrugged his shoulders before he continued to stroll away.

Follow him, boy.

"We don't even know where we are."

Exactly.

He has the answers we need.

I looked back down the alley towards Joseph St. Claire, who had just turned the corner out. With no other options, and against my better judgment, I chased after the strange man.

* * * * * * *

JOSEPH ST. CLAIRE DISAPPEARED. I TURNED THE corner just seconds after him but he was already gone. People crowded the street beyond the alley, blocking my view as I looked around for the man. I tried to spot his insane outfit in the crowd but there was no sign of him anywhere. He had vanished.

We need to find him.

"Yeah, no shit," I said as I pushed my way through a crowd of people. "What does this guy want with you, anyway? Why the hell did he bring us here?"

I don't know, though I believe he's the Oracle.

I slowed down, recalling that Joseph had called himself that earlier. I finally recognized a term in this crazy new world I found myself in. I had read about oracles somewhere before. "Do you mean, like, from antiquity?"

You know that word?

"Okay, man. What is that supposed to mean?"

Nothing, nothing.

Just surprising, that's all.

LORDAL

"You know what? Fuck you." Lordal decided to carry on with the conversation, ignoring my insult.

Yes, boy. The same Oracle.

There is only one.

Mankind has greatly exaggerated the role, but yes.

I was still looking for a way to get above the crowd. The streets were flooded with people for some reason. "Tell me about it then," I said. "We've got the time. I'll keep looking for this guy."

I don't know much.

"I don't know anything."

Right.

Well, the Oracle is a celestial entity.

Though it isn't immortal.

It chooses a willing host —

"That's nice. I didn't ask for you."

...and remains until the end of the host's life.

"Until it needs a new host. I guess I'm lucky you make me immortal."

You aren't.

Someone can kill you if they're creative enough.

I would come back.

"I wouldn't," I said as I pushed my way through the crowd. I let out a long breath of cool air. "Gotcha."

The Oracle also can't use its gift to benefit itself.

"What does that mean?"

Joseph St. Claire doesn't know how, or when, he'll die.

He can't see his own future.

"So... What? None of this explains what the Oracle wants with you," I said as I turned the corner into another alley.

LORDAL

It may need help with something, perhaps some sort of task.

It's called upon warriors to aid it throughout time.

This is how I know its existence to be true.

Find Joseph St. Claire, and we'll find the Oracle.

* * * * * * *

I GAVE UP MY SEARCH WHEN I FOUND THE FREE tequila. It was shortly after it started being offered that I learned I was teleported from the redwood forests of Northern California to the heart of Mexico City, and that it was Cinco de Mayo. I could hardly remember what day it was when this nightmare started. Now I was eight shots deep from the bottle of tequila I was carrying in my hand, laughing at myself for not noticing everyone was speaking Spanish sooner.

"I say we go south, head down to Central America," I slurred to Lordal. I had managed to find my way into a relatively empty plaza, where I was leaning against a brick wall to stay on my feet. It was hard to remember my life before Lordal, so it was hard to remember anything but awful, horrible times. Already so much had changed, and this seemed to be the direction my life was taking me. Only I didn't have a life anymore, I thought silently. There was nothing left for me back home. Everything was different now. Being wasted in the middle of Mexico was the first time I was in a good mood in... I couldn't even recall how long, only that it had been weeks now.

We can't leave.

The Oracle wants us here for a reason.

The balance may be in question.

"The balance?" I busted out laughing. "Balance of what?"

Winded from my laughter I sat down, setting my tequila bottle down on the ground beside me. Luckily, I was drunk, so no one questioned the guy laughing to himself. To the people watching me, I was just another drunken fool celebrating a bit too much.

My thoughts drifted back to that first night. I saw Tyson's body in front of me—his betrayed eyes, his heart in my hands—and shook it out of my head. My stomach turned and my face sank. I wouldn't allow myself to go back into those memories. I took a few deep breaths to calm myself, then raised an imaginary glass in the air. "Well, at least I can still get drunk. Amen."

Don't start crying, boy.

"Shut the fuck up, Lordal."

You're insufferable.

"Yeah? Well, you're—"

I stopped as I felt shaking beneath me. I got to my feet, panicked by the sudden thought of an earthquake. The sound of shattering glass came from beside me and I groaned to myself in an exaggerated manner, knowing it could only be my bottle of tequila that had broken.

The ground shook violently again, knocking me off my feet. I caught myself against the wall, steadying myself before looking back to search the plaza for the source of the chaos. There was a loud banging sound, like pipes being struck against each other, coming from beneath the earth. I struggled back onto my feet just as the ground exploded upward in front of me. Below, I could just make out the structures of a massive sewer system — and something making its way out.

I was one tequila shot away from blackout drunk. I was in no condition to be dealing with a Mexican sewer monster.

Debris fell all around me as I inched my way forward, toward the gaping hole in the center of the plaza. Something shifted as I moved closer, scratching at the concrete like a dog at a door. The clawing stopped, only to be followed by a guttural howl that echoed through the plaza. Somewhere in that time, my mind decided to become sober again.

"What the fuck is that?" I whispered as I tripped over a brick and stumbled forward a few feet. The banging sound picked back up, this time slowly but much, much louder.

Anthony, wait.

"What's the big deal? What are you afraid of, man? Did you forget?" I slammed my fist against my chest one time to embolden myself. "Unkillable, remember?"

Not unkillable, you worthless drunk.

You just spent days dying in the woods.

"Oh, right. Fuck."

I was knocked back down on my ass by another minor earthquake. Ahead, something leapt out from the hole in the ground. A massive shadow was cast as it flew overhead, before it landed a few yards behind me. A chilling howl filled the air, widening my eyes before I slowly turned my head to look at it. A massive dog-like beast sniffed the air. I watched as the creature stretched its body in front of me, its muscles flexing and bulging under its thick blood-stained fur. It sniffed the ground where I had sat only moments ago, then rose back up and stalked forward one giant paw after the other toward me. Its fangs were bigger than my hands, and its eyes had a beautiful golden glow in the sun. They remained fixated on only one thing.

Run, you fool!

"Holy shit," I said as I stared into the beast's golden eyes. I began to back up slowly, my heartbeat increasing with every step. There was no direction I could go that would get me away from this beast. "What the fuck is that?"

Before Lordal could respond, I bumped into someone with my back who had my answer. "It's a hellhound," said Joseph, pushing me aside. "It's been sent to kill you. Or maybe it's here for me. Let's find out, shall we?"

Joseph held a lever-action rifle. I ducked as he aimed, hitting the ground with my elbows as he opened fire. The creature snarled, backing up before turning and sprinting off into the marketplace where I'd gotten the tequila earlier. It leapt up, using the walls to reach the rooftops. Joseph lowered his rifle and watched it run off before extending a hand to help me to my feet. "Thanks," I said. "What was that thing?"

"I told you. It's a hellhound. They've been very problematic lately."

I couldn't tell if he meant problematic during his own lifetime or if it was the Oracle speaking. I didn't understand what he was, or how he worked.

"Is that why you brought us here?" I asked.

Joseph nodded his head as he slung his rifle over his shoulder. "Not quite, though I'd appreciate your help."

"It was coming for me but it didn't attack. It must be after you, right? Or…" I trailed off, trying to piece it all together as if I understood anything about anything going on anymore. Then something Lordal had said about the Oracle came back to me. I turned back to Joseph. "Mr. St. Claire, what is going on? Lordal said something about a 'balance in question'? Look, I don't want any part of this, okay? Can we just get this over with?"

"You don't need to call me 'Mister,'" he said with a charming smile and soft chuckle. "Joseph is fine, or St. Claire."

I crouched down next to the massive hole in the ground leading into the sewer system, resting my head in my hand while I looked down. I stared at it as if it were my invisible puzzle, but I still hadn't found any of the pieces I needed to finish it. I looked back up at Joseph before rising to my feet. "Okay, Joseph. What do you know that I don't?"

"Come with me." Joseph placed a hand on my shoulder. "Please, I insist. I'll explain what I can."

* * * * * * *

"WHERE EXACTLY ARE WE GOING, JOSEPH?" I asked, finally putting the most obvious question out there. I'd followed the man maybe six blocks before deciding to ask. There hadn't been a word between us the entire time, not that it surprised me much. I had no idea where we were going or what he seemed to be looking for. It was apparent to me that the Oracle believed everyone was on a sort of need-to-know basis.

"I need to find a suitable door. Sorry. I'm rather particular about this sort of thing," he responded, looking over his shoulder. He had done so at the end of every street. I didn't know if it was because he wanted to make sure I was still with him or if he wanted to make sure the hellhound wasn't still following us.

I was beginning to understand that sometimes Joseph spoke about himself as the Oracle, and sometimes he just meant himself, his human identity. I understood his situation, though I was jealous of his possession. He accepted the Oracle, and they seemed to be one. Lordal and I were stuck with each other, and we'd each prefer the other gone.

"What's so special about a door?" I asked, pushing my way through the crowd to keep up with him. Joseph seemed to know exactly when and where to step, seamlessly weaving his way through the flood of people celebrating in the streets. It took all my focus just to keep up with him.

"If I pick the wrong door..." He shook his head as he seemed to remember it happening. "I once chose poorly, a long time ago. Made a small wormhole. It wasn't on purpose but it did destroy an entire city on the seabed of the Atlantic Ocean. Then I once found myself in the Pacific Ocean, and that was a whole another mess, too. They ended up calling that... What was it? Marias... Mabillia..."

"You mean the Mariana Trench? You did that?"

"Yes! Yes, that's it." He snapped his fingers, satisfied with his jogged memory.

Joseph St. Claire was far too young to have created the Mariana Trench, so I knew I was talking to the Oracle. It was fascinating to me how they blended into one being.

"You mentioned a city on the seabed…" I started.

I remember Atlantis.

Great place.

"Atlantis?" I shouted in astonishment, forgetting only I could hear Lordal.

"Yes! Yes, it was called Atlantis. It was beautiful. Such a shame what happened to it, but I learned my lesson."

Joseph smiled fondly with what appeared to be pleasant memories while I followed closely behind. I was steadily growing concerned with the Oracle's nonchalant attitude. It seemed like a god compared to Lordal. I needed to learn more about what it knew, including its knowledge about the demon inside me. Maybe it could give me the answers I needed. "Have you met before?" I asked. "You and Lordal, I mean. Was 'Lordal and the Oracle' ever a thing?"

"We have met, though not to the demon's knowledge. His destiny is far too significant for me to pay him no mind."

I don't like what he just said.

I ignored Lordal to listen to the Oracle.

"The clock will stop soon," the Oracle continued. "I needed to check on his development to make sure we're prepared."

"Prepared for what? These hellhounds?"

"For war."

The Oracle spoke how Lordal did, vaguely — annoyingly — but I wasn't going to pester an entity after it told me of all the devastation it caused accidentally. I couldn't imagine pissing it off and seeing what it could do intentionally.

"What about Joseph? Are you like me? I mean, how Lordal and I—"

"No," said Joseph. There was suddenly a human emotion in his tone. I could notice the change from Oracle to host. "I'm simply a vessel," Joseph continued. "I'm me until the Oracle wishes to speak and I allow it to. I'm merely a messenger. It's always a choice. I always say yes."

Must be nice.

We're not so bad, you and I.

Speak for yourself.

"Why did you become the Oracle's host?" I asked, ignoring the pestering demon inside once more.

"I couldn't sit on the sidelines when I knew what was coming. What is coming, and that I can still do something about it before it all burns. Lives are at stake. Countless lives." The thoughts that came with those words clearly troubled him, if only enough for a moment of pause.

"But doesn't it ever seem too much? I'm still having a hard time wrapping my head around it all. Demons and devils, and now I'm with you and you can see the future. It's chaos all the time."

"It exists. You exist in it now. Don't overcomplicate it," he said with a shrug. "Everyone figures out how to deal with it their own way. You just have to remember; you have the same choice I do. You need to decide where you stand in this insanity, just as much as Lordal does."

I understood what Joseph meant but our possessions weren't anywhere near the same. I didn't have the same choice as him. He chose to be the Oracle's host. I woke up one day with a monster in my head. It made me do things I still wish never happened. There was a difference and Joseph couldn't see it.

We walked in silence for the rest of the way. I enjoyed the sights and sounds of the festivities. Joseph slowed down enough for me to walk next to him. We walked for three more blocks before he pointed out a building and we made our way to it. He led me up the short staircase to a massive double-doored building. The doors were beautifully crafted. They were a deep olive-green with polished knockers on each side, though what stood out most were the giant curved handles in the shape of scaled wings. "Do you see them?" Joseph asked, staring at the doors.

"Yes. Is that bad?"

"It's great," he said as he walked up. "It means you're allowed to enter."

Joseph pulled open one of the doors, straining with the weight at first. I was ready for another mind-blowing magical reveal but what I saw was a poorly furnished entryway to a run-down apartment building. Joseph smiled, holding the door open for me.

"This is the place?" I tried hiding my disappointment.

"Don't sound so disappointed! Come on, go in. If you thought things were crazy before, you're not ready for this."

"Really, man? Is that what you think?" I said, tilting my head to get a better look inside. "Hate to break it to you, dude, but I don't think anything about this place is going to blow my mind."

"Come on, are you serious? Fine. Watch this." Joseph stepped through the doorway, vanishing the moment he passed the threshold.

"Alright. That was pretty fucking cool," I mumbled. "So, uh… What the hell was that?"

Who cares?

Follow him, boy.

We must learn what he knows.

"Right," I said, rolling my eyes. "Let's just blindly walk through the doors that defy the laws of physics. That's cool." I stuck my hand through the doorway. Nothing happened.

Go boy.

Follow him.

Hesitantly, I took another step forward, setting my right foot over the threshold. It remained fully visible, still attached to the rest of my body.

Follow him, boy!

I tire of your fear.

"I don't know," I said, rubbing my chin. "Where the fuck did he go?" Lordal seemed to keep forgetting that this was all very new to me. Everything about this supernatural world was terrifying. What if I walked through and came out the other end a butterfly? How was I supposed to know what was safe and what was going to kill me?

If it was going to kill you it would have by now, fool!

Now go, before I go for you!

I rolled my eyes at the demon's tantrum as I stepped through and vanished.

* * * * * * *

"WHAT THE HELL JUST HAPPENED?" I ASKED UPON entering an entirely blank space. The room was a familiar void—darkness, emptiness—for only a moment. Before I could question what was happening, a purple carpet began to materialize beneath my feet. Then came a solid wooden floor, then pots filled with strange yet beautiful flowers appeared to my left and right, until an entirely new entryway had replaced the rundown apartment building from only moments earlier.

"That's pretty fucking cool," I said again as I watched staircases spiral into existence and extend up to the heavens. Columns of black marble formed from dust, supporting a towering ceiling. The tapestry above us displayed the night sky, and a symbol of an eye with a teardrop for the pupil rested in the middle of it all, watching over the entryway.

"More to your liking, I assume?" said Joseph, appearing at the top of one of the staircases, walking down to me.

"What is this place?"

"I simply call it the Oracle's Manor. It's linked to me, for as long as I'm its host." He pointed behind me. "Look."

I turned to see that the beautiful doors were gone, replaced by a swirling mass of stars and stardust, glimmering like they do in images of galaxies.

"We're in a dimension just outside of the known universe," said Joseph as he came up to stand beside me. He placed a reassuring hand on my shoulder. "We'll be safe here. Nothing can breach those doors."

Joseph turned away, heading toward another set of doors which swung open gently as he approached. "Now that you're here, I need to show you something."

"Something cooler than this?"

"I never said it was 'cool.'" His tone had gotten quite serious.

"Oh." I paused, then began to follow him further into the manor. "Well then, what is it?"

"The darkest of futures."

Oh, that is cool.

* * * * * * *

"TIME PASSES DIFFERENTLY HERE," JOSEPH explained as he led me through the manor, "adjacent to the mortal world you know."

The manor was massive. We passed several rooms on our way through its halls. I looked into whichever had a door open and each was its own pocket of space and time. Two had completely different environments and climates in them, filled with strange and exotic animals I had never seen before and would most likely never see again. One was mostly empty, save for a single clock with a strange circular symbol carved into its face. Its hands were ticking away, echoing in the empty space. There was one with rows of slabs and names engraved upon them, like a memorial site — or a graveyard. I couldn't ignore the chill that ran up my spine as we passed that room.

"It bends to my will, yet I have no idea how to control it," Joseph continued as we entered another room. Treasures from across time decorated the space. Troves of priceless artifacts glimmered around us. Paintings decorated the walls, none of which I recognized. Yet I knew instantly that gazing upon them was surely sin, for they were without comparison to anything I had ever seen before, or would possibly ever see again.

"I'm still new to all of this for the most part," Joseph kept going. My gaze broke away from the masterpieces. Joseph waved his hand around the room, scratching the back of his neck. "I never expected this to be my life. My fate, if you want to be dramatic about it."

"I know what you mean," I said quietly. "Sometimes I can feel myself slipping away, losing myself to Lordal. There's never any control for me. If that's how it is for you, then I understand."

"It's not like that. That's not what I mean at all," said Joseph with a chuckle. "The Oracle isn't fighting for control over its host, and it means well. It's not a rageful demon inside me. The Oracle's a guiding force. If I chose to abandon its mission, it would simply wait until I passed to find its next vessel."

Joseph led me further into the room. In the center was a low coffee table surrounded by six chairs, all crafted of a beautiful metal I had never seen before. It was strangely social for someone I couldn't imagine having visitors.

"It all feels so familiar, yet I don't recognize any of it. Please," he said, gesturing toward a chair. As I sat down, Joseph said, "Come to think of it, you never got to properly introduce yourself. What's your name, kid?"

Don't answer that.

"Right," I said, ignoring the annoying intruder in my mind. "Sorry. I didn't even realize."

"Well, we were in quite a rush to get here."

"I'm Anthony," I finally told him, extending my hand. "Anthony Monroe."

"It's a pleasure," said Joseph, shaking my hand before walking away to rummage through shelves and drawers.

"So, you're connected to this place?" I asked, still gawking at the marvels around us. There were relics from across ages, from civilizations lost long ago, and others seemingly from other worlds. Each piece demanded my attention. I wondered silently to myself if any of it was from Atlantis. "You're connected to all of this?"

"In a way," said Joseph, his voice snapping me out of my daze for a moment. He was across the room, still rummaging through the various artifacts. Above us, beautiful stained-glass windows revealed the endless void outside. Stars twinkled in the darkness. I was staring into the void while Joseph rambled on, no longer paying attention to him.

Joseph pulled out a thick book bound in old leather and slammed it down on the table in front of me. Dust bounced off of it from the impact, though he was unfazed as he wiped it clean with a rag. I stared at the book, compelled to reach out toward it.

"What is this?" I asked as I picked up the book.

Joseph shrugged as I undid the knot tying it shut. "An ancient text, one connected to the very being that cursed your demon," he explained. "Not even the Oracle seems to understand it. I was hoping Lordal could tell me what it says."

What? Why?

I flipped through the pages, expecting to be awestruck. Instead, I was greeted by strange symbols filling up whole pages from front to back. It looked handwritten; each symbol so carefully detailed. Whoever had written the book had gone through a great deal to make it understandable, at least to anyone that could read it. I could feel Lordal's intrigue, and I could feel his disappointment at the emptiness it brought him as well.

I don't know what this is.

I shook my head, shutting the giant paperweight and placing it back on the table. "Sorry, man. He doesn't know what this thing is either. Is this why you brought us here?"

"The Oracle brought you here."

"Do you know why?" I pointed at the book. "What is this thing? What're all those symbols in there?"

Joseph shrugged as he picked up the book again, throwing it back on the shelf he found it on. "I told you. I don't know. Perhaps its connection with Lucifer is why the Oracle thought Lordal may be able to decipher it."

I could feel Lordal's curiosity as if it were burning a hole in my brain. Joseph stepped through a side door then, returning a moment later with a bowl of fruit that he placed on the table. He picked up an apple and bit into it. He pushed the bowl toward me. When I politely refused, he shrugged and closed his eyes while he chewed, deep in thought.

"Why am I here, Joseph? What's going on? You whisked me into a whole different country to read a book?"

Joseph swallowed his mouthful of apple, then held up a finger like a teacher would. "You ask a lot of questions."

I stood up, slamming my fists on the table as flames leapt from them, like the dust had off the book. "And you seem useless for an all-seeing entity's host!" I was fully aware of my rage as I leaned forward. "Why did you bring me here?"

Joseph tossed his apple aside, locking eyes with me as we stared across the table at each other. We stood there for a moment—for long enough that I remembered who I was threatening, what he could do. Luckily, Joseph was unfazed by my outburst. He remained completely calm. He pointed at the chair behind me and said, "Sit down, Anthony."

I did so reluctantly. The look in his eyes told me it could have been the last thing I ever heard if I didn't. Joseph sighed, taking a seat across from me. He crossed one leg over the other and leaned back in his chair, looking out of a window into the void. His expression changed to one of sorrow before he spoke again. "I'll start from the beginning," he said, resting his hands on the table as his gaze turned from the starlit abyss to me. "This all started about three weeks ago now. The night I became the Oracle."

"You've only been the Oracle for three weeks?" I tried not to sound too surprised but the way he smiled told me I failed completely.

"Yes," he said with a nod of his head. "That's how it works. When one Oracle dies, another rises to take the mantle. Every Oracle knows the previous in some way. The Oracle before me was my fiancée, Elizabeth."

I was still processing the fact that Joseph had been the Oracle for less time than I had been Lordal's host. Then I realized what he said and my heart broke for the man. Elizabeth was dead, obviously, or I would be talking to her instead of him right now. "I'm sorry," I said quietly.

Joseph gave me a soft smile before he shook his head. It clearly hurt, and it would for the rest of his days, but he was trying to move forward. I thought of Tyson then and felt a kinship with Joseph St. Claire. Two hosts, two great losses.

Were you and the boy engaged as well?

Shut up, Lordal.

I could feel Lordal's pleasure in teasing me. "Why did you become the Oracle?" I asked Joseph. "I mean, after—"

"I don't know. The universe works in mysterious ways. Things have now been set in motion that even the Oracle cannot foresee. Though I do know what took my beloved Elizabeth, and I knew the Oracle's gift could help me avenge her."

The hellhound.

They only bring carnage wherever they go.

"The hellhound," I repeated Lordal's words out loud. "It killed her."

"Yes, the same beast from today," said Joseph as he stared back off at the stars outside again, replaying it all in his head. "It found us when we arrived in Mexico City. It tore her to shreds and left me for dead. I woke up later with these visions in here," he waved his hand next to his head. "I can still feel her. Her thoughts. Her love... But she's gone now."

Silence fell over us for a moment as Joseph recomposed himself. He closed his eyes, took a deep breath, then turned to me. "None of that matters now. I can see that clearly, and she knew it too. We've always known. My personal agenda aside, a greater cause requires our attention."

I looked at him curiously, aware that the Oracle was speaking to me now. "What is it you've always known?"

"There is a war coming, Anthony Monroe, between Earth and Hell, and the Heavens have no intention of playing a part," the Oracle explained. "We are horribly unprepared. The world hasn't seen the supernatural in over a millennia."

"So, what?" I said slowly, trying to process what I was hearing. "I'm, like, the chosen one?"

The Oracle shook his head. "No, Anthony Monroe. Not you. I didn't even know your name until moments ago. I have never seen your future. I don't know what it holds for you, though I do believe you will be Lordal's host in this time of conflict."

What is he talking about?

"What do you need Lordal for?" I asked, putting a hand on my head to keep it from spinning. I was suddenly very dizzy.

"Lordal's destiny. I have always known it. I have always seen it. The demon that will take the throne and free the realm of Hell from the hands of Lucifer."

Ah, I see now.

Lucifer is a part of this.

There was something about the way Lordal said the name, a familiarity. There was an anger to it. A flame flickered inside me briefly. I stood up and began pacing back and forth. "You mean, like, Lucifer? Like, the Devil? Satan himself?"

Joseph got to his feet as well and made his way back to the door we entered from. "Come," he called for me. "It's simpler if I just show you."

"What does Lordal have to do with all of this?" I asked, chasing him out into the hallways. "This is insane! You want me to, what? Go kill the Devil? Where? In Hell?"

Joseph shook his head as he continued to stroll down the hall. "No. We can do better than that."

"Yeah? How's that?" I asked as I leaned back against the wall, trying to catch my breath as the room started to spin. I was on the brink of a panic attack. Or maybe I was already having one. It was really hard to tell what was going on inside my head at this point. There was definitely too much going on right now. I didn't know where to begin with it all.

"Only Lordal needs to descend into Hell," Joseph started. "We can separate you. Your curse can be lifted."

I snapped my head toward him. "What?"

Joseph stopped, turning back to look at me. "We can separate you. Or rather, Luka can."

There was that name again. The shadow man—no, the phantom figure. "And where is he?"

"He'll be here when we need him."

"Don't we need him now?"

Don't sound so desperate, boy.

Joseph turned and strolled off again.

"Don't bullshit me, Joseph!" I called after him. Just as I did, he ducked into one of the doors we had passed on our way to the back of the manor.

Follow him, you fool.

"How about you tell me why he seems to think you're going to kill the Devil?"

It is my only goal.

My only purpose.

"What?" I shouted, looking around as if there was someone around to share my surprise. "Do you understand how insane that sounds?"

Lucifer did this to me.

I swore that I would kill him for it.

Holy fuck.

The demon inside me had a personal vendetta with Lucifer, the Devil himself. I ran after Joseph, still struggling to process everything. I turned into the door that he had gone through and found him inside a room I peeked in earlier. Joseph was staring at the clock with the pentagram carved into its face. The clock itself was a masterwork. I was moving too fast to notice before that its body was made up of monsters and angels circling up from the base, toward the ticking hands of its face. The pentagram was glowing now, which it wasn't doing earlier. "It's called the Hands of the Apocalypse," said Joseph, answering my question before I could ask. "I have no idea who or what created it, or where it came from. It predates my existence. I only know that it shows how much time your world has left."

"I'm guessing it's not much." I stepped up next to him. "You know, for someone who's supposed to see the future and everything, you're pretty bad at it."

"This was here before me. I cannot see events that occurred before my time." The Oracle grabbed my arm then, holding it up in the air between us. I cried out as a symbol burned into my flesh, lines slashed together into an unfamiliar mark. "You have no idea the power inside you, boy," he boomed, throwing my arm down. I yanked it to my chest, looking at the mark burned into my wrist. Lordal's power couldn't heal it away. "You're a vessel for something far more powerful than you can ever imagine."

"Clearly not as powerful as you," I said through gritted teeth. "What did you do to me?"

"I've prepared you for your journey," he told me, looking at the clock. "It's not you I need right now."

"What are you talking about?" I asked as a blue fog began to swirl around me, immediately obscuring my vision. "Where are we going? What's happening? What did you do to me?"

"Only you're going, Anthony," said the Oracle. "If you are to help us, you must see the truth. This is his destiny, so it will be yours."

I choked on the blue fog as it reached my lungs. It brought me to my knees. My eyes were watering as I tried to call out but I had no voice to speak. I collapsed to the ground as the world faded away, until there was only the dense blue fog and the ticking of the Hands of the Apocalypse.

* * * * * * *

I TOOK DEEP BREATHS OF AIR AS THE BLUE FOG shifted away, only to cough it all out. I had inhaled thick smoke. The fog vanished and the world took shape around me, revealing a smoldering forest caught in flames. I scrambled backwards as burning branches fell from above, nearly killing me before I could figure out why I was here. Could I even die? I wasn't clear on what was happening, or where I was. The Oracle's doing, no doubt.

Birds scattered overhead, spreading their wings amongst the flames in an attempt to save themselves. Then a bloodcurdling scream echoed after them, sending a chill down my spine. I walked into a clearing as a roar, more animal-like in nature, followed. I crouched behind the burning brush, unsure where these sounds were coming from. They were close though, and I didn't want to risk being found. The thick smoke had covered the meadow now but I could still make out the two figures that entered the clearing I found myself in. The flames leapt from tree to tree around them as they circled, locked in a violent struggle that had clearly caused this forest fire. I crawled closer, hoping to see, but the smoke was only getting thicker. The man became clear as I crawled out from the brush behind him. He was clothed in hides and furs of several creatures, clothing from whatever time this was. He was dark and muscular, and stood well over six feet tall. He held a spear in his hands, aimed at his opponent's direction across the clearing. They couldn't see any better than I could through all this smoke. I couldn't make out the other combatant, but I saw as they charged at each other, tackled each other to the ground. The man with the spear was using it to defend himself from a creature. It had glowing red eyes and black fur matted by blood. Fire blew past its mouth when it breathed. Its muscles bulged under its skin. It howled in victory like a wolf to the moon.

    I recognized the creature. It was a hellhound, though not the same one that had attacked me in Mexico City. I could also see now that the man was badly injured. His blood was pooling beneath him, seeping into the ground, staining the flowers. The hellhound had done its worst, and the man had done his best. The beast stopped howling, snapping its head around, raising it, then sniffing the air. It growled when it was done, lowering its face down to the look into the man's eyes. "You are alone," it stated, its voice deep and commanding. It blinked slowly, much slower than a human. That was somehow the most unsettling thing about it.

    "You speak, demon?" the man asked through gritted teeth. He wasn't the only one confused by this fact. Until now, the only demon I had heard speak was Lordal, and that was only in my head.

"Yes," it said. Its tail flicked in amusement, less like a hound and more like the lion before it devoured the gazelle. "You are Orm Gon? Slayer of Demons? Hunter of the Night Creatures?"

"I am he," said Orm Gon. "I am glad you will know the name of the man that sends you to your grave."

"You are dying, fool." The hound reared its head back, cackling. It looked back down at Orm Gon. "How will you defeat me when you can no longer stand?"

"My Lord will aid me in your destruction, of this I—"

The demon dove back into his face, its jaws snapping loudly. "Like I said, fool," each word came out like a growl as it spoke, "you are alone. There is no God here. Just you, me, and the flames that surround us." The hellhound dug its claws into Orm's chest, causing him to scream in pain. "Do you think your God would let me kill you if He loved you?"

"God loves all his creatures," Orm shouted in agony as the demon raked its claws down his leg, tearing it open. I gagged as the bone became visible.

"He never loved me." The demon clicked its tongue, as if in thought. "I'm going to kill you," it decided suddenly. "Tell your God when you reach Him that it was Lucifer who killed you."

The beast suddenly burst into flames, transforming within the fire to take the form of an entirely nude man. Lucifer emerged from the flames; his massive black-feathered wings extended from his shoulder blades. The fallen angel was a beautiful specimen. His sword hung from his side, held in place by a belt made of his feathers. His hair was long and ravenous, black and greasy like oil. I was enthralled by his handsome face, for I had never seen such beauty. His wings suddenly folded around him to conceal his nudity, covering him like armor. It seemed even the Devil had a sense of modesty. Lucifer grabbed the dying man by his throat, hoisting him to his feet and looking him in the eyes. "Do you still believe your God loves you, Orm Gon?"

Orm couldn't speak. He was being strangled. I saw myself for a moment, amongst the redwoods, choking the dying hunter. I shuddered at the comparison.

Lucifer regarded the shriveling crippled form of the man he now held limply in his hand. "Why would He love a liar? You know as well as I do, there's no such thing as demons." Lucifer spoke softly, talking calmly to Orm Gon. He brought his face closer to the man's. "Only the Devil."

Lucifer tightened his grip, watching the light die in Orm's eyes. "Please…" Orm managed to gasp, grabbing hold of the Devil's arm. "I do not wish to die."

I remembered the hunter again, begging for mercy. I shook my head. That wasn't why I was sent here.

Lucifer broke his gaze to look at Orm's hands on his arm, staring at them as they struggled to loosen the Devil's grip. Lucifer suddenly flicked his wrist, slamming Orm into a tree. Orm crumpled. His head lowered to his chest. The Devil stepped over him, held his head up by his hair, and smashed his other fist into his face, over and over. There were no screams, no cries for mercy. Just the sound of Orm's face being smashed in as the Devil's fist continued to come down on him. The sound of his skull breaking was heard over the crackle of flames around us. The brutality of the sight made me sick to my stomach.

I suddenly remembered that none of this was real. That Joseph St. Claire had sent me here to see this. It calmed me down slightly, though I didn't understand what the Oracle wanted me to see. The Devil was vile—I could have guessed that without this crazy trip.

Lucifer suddenly lowered his fist. Somehow, Orm was still breathing, if only barely. Lucifer crouched down to look at the man's destroyed face—eyes bulging out of their sockets, some teeth swallowed, some barely hanging on, and some shattered to pieces in his mouth. His nose was caved in. He was a broken man, bloodied and beaten. Lucifer was still holding his head back with a firm grip of his hair. He pulled it back again, causing Orm obvious pain, as he said, "No one's love is unconditional, not even God's. I wouldn't be here if it was."

"Please," Orm barely managed to gurgle out.

"I can make you like me, a celestial being beyond your understanding."

The dying man's eyes widened as he drew his last breath. I shook my head silently, begging him not to go through with it. I finally understood what I was watching. Why I was here. I knew in my heart what was about to happen.

"What can you give me, Orm Gon?"

"Everything," said Orm, his final words as a mortal man. "I will give you everything."

I watched as the Devil grinned over Orm's dying body. This dying man, I knew him already. He wasn't shown to me by mistake. This was the beginning of what would eventually become my own nightmare. Orm Gon was Lordal, before the curse had changed the course of his life. The realization rocked me. He hadn't been some hero. He wasn't a savior that made the ultimate sacrifice. He was a coward, and a liar, too afraid to die like anyone else.

If only I could warn him now of the lifetimes of misery he would endure. If only I could tell him that the Devil would not turn him into a great being of power but a demon, a creature forever despised on this Earth. No one deserved that fate. Maybe Lucifer was right. Maybe the Lord's love wasn't unconditional. Maybe some people were just damned.

The Devil raised his hand to the air, examining it as his eyes turned black like the limbo's abyss, and wicked claws grew from his fingertips. He turned his gaze back down to Orm Gon. "Surrender your soul to me, mortal. It is all I require if you are to live."

He said it so calmly, without a doubt that Orm would do as he was told. The Devil began to carve a symbol in his other hand with his claws. I was too far to make it out. When he was done, his claws returned into his fingertips, and he lowered the bleeding hand down to the dying man. I looked down at my wrist, where the Oracle had marked me, once I could see the mark the Devil carved into himself. It was the same symbol: the Mark of Lordal.

Lucifer drew his sword from his side, extending it toward Orm Gon with his other hand. I shook my head in disappointment as Orm reached for the blade, dragging his hand across it. Even as he was dying, Lucifer and I both noticed the briefest moment of hesitation, but I already knew what would happen. It had already happened. There was no changing it now. Orm Gon reached out and grasped the Devil's hand in his own. Flames leapt from Lucifer's skin, coming alive the moment he and Orm made contact. I watched the flames dance across his body, twirling around his arms before reaching Orm's. Then the flames changed, springing forward violently, latching onto the man's skin, tearing him apart. Orm began to scream, but was silenced by the emergence of a thick blue smoke seeping slowly out of his mouth. I could only assume it was his soul. It danced above his body, stretching out into the sky, only to be yanked back by Lucifer. He coiled it around his free hand, like cotton candy on a stick.

Orm watched in terror as the flames consumed him. He stared at his soul, which was now completely in the hands of Lucifer. The Devil flicked his hand, then the soul burned away until there was nothing left.

"The deal is done. Your soul is mine," said Lucifer. I suddenly heard Lordal echo the same words to me in my head, when he first took control. "You will walk this Earth in the minds of man until I have need of you," Lucifer continued. "You are an undying parasite. Death will never take you. You are of hellfire now. Feel it consume you. Feel it engrave its power into your being. Feel it become your soul. You are part of me, blessed with my power. You are my herald on this Earth. Now burn."

The flames intensified. Orm's screams filled the air in his transformation from man to demon. Before he died his first death, he took one last look at the Devil, staring him in the eyes. Orm struggled to speak as he burned. He shook his head, accepting his damnation. Before the flames destroyed him entirely, he spoke to Lucifer one last time. His rage was familiar suddenly—Orm Gon was now Lordal.

"You watch me burn now, Devil," said Lordal. "One day, I'll watch you burn just the same." Then he screamed once more as he died by hellfire. The first death of many.

Lucifer released the charred corpse's hand, leaving Orm's remains in the dirt.

The world shifted around me. It was over. I had seen what I was sent here to see. The burning forest faded away, then Lucifer, then Orm's remains. It felt as if I was being pulled through water, then I felt the familiar sensation of floating as the same blue fog took me again.

LORDAL

MY HEAD BANGED AGAINST A WINDOW AS I jolted awake. I groaned as it throbbed in pain, then I sat up and wiped the drool from my mouth. "Where the hell are we?" I asked St. Claire, who was driving the Jeep. We were driving down an old dirt road with abandoned factories all around us.

"Welcome back. Lordal, I assume?" he said, his eyes on the road. "I was wondering when you would take control."

I looked out the window, up at the sun high above. It seemed no time had passed at all since we entered the Manor, though it could have been days. "When did we leave the Manor?" I asked, sinking back into my seat.

"Only minutes ago. Carrying you into the Jeep was a hassle. Anthony is heavier than you'd think." St. Claire seemed distant when he spoke, almost out of sync with the world around him.

"What did you do to him?"

"Anthony is... He's elsewhere." He gestured with his hand as he spoke, fluttering it to the side before tapping the side of his head. "Deeper within your shared consciousness."

"And us?" I asked, watching the mundane scenery pass us by. "Where are you taking us?"

St. Claire slowed to a stop then, parking in a random spot on the road. He looked around, then blinked a few times before rubbing his hand over his face and looking over at me. "Here," he said as if he was surprised by his decision. "I'm taking us here."

We were on a back road, where delivery trucks would drive if any of these buildings were still operational. It looked like they had all shut down years ago.

"You ask a lot of questions too," said St. Claire as he stepped out of the Jeep. He made his way to the trunk.

I hopped out and looked around while he rummaged through his supplies. There was nothing interesting about our location, just a bunch of decrepit empty factories and warehouses. I moved to the back of the Jeep, turning the corner to see St. Claire loading a shotgun. He put extra shells in his shoulder bag. I pointed at the weapon in his hands. "What has the Oracle shown you, St. Claire? Why are we here?"

"Men are going to die soon." He pulled on a green cargo jacket, every pocket filled with his necessary tools and traps. He closed the trunk and pointed at the nearest building. "They're under that one, working in the sewers."

"What does this have to do with us?" I asked, looking at the old factory. "Men die every minute of every day."

St. Claire walked into the alleyway alongside the building, not bothering to turn back as he said, "We're here for what kills them."

Joseph St. Claire wasn't here to save these men. He accepted their fate. He wasn't trying to change it. I sniffed the air, catching the familiar scent of the hellhound.

The screaming started seconds later, coming from around the side of the building. We looked at each other for a moment before running off in the direction. As we rounded the corner, St. Claire quickly held out an arm to stop me from falling forward as we reached a gaping hole in the ground. "It's down there," he started. "Listen to me, Lordal. We can't kill it."

Without the boy's presence, my blood was already starting to boil. "What the hell are you on about? Do you understand what that thing is?" I paused, exhaled some heat. I needed to stay calm. "Why are we here if we aren't going to kill it?"

St. Claire reached into one of his pockets and pulled out a small device that looked like a needle with a blinking green light on one end. "This is going to lead us to wherever that hellhound came from," he explained. "I need to stab this into it. Or get it to eat it, so long as it's on or inside that thing."

"Neither will be easy," I said quietly as I walked up to the gaping hole. St. Claire returned the tracking device to his pocket as I passed him.

"We can't kill it, Lordal," he repeated, though I knew this time it was the Oracle. I understood. The good Oracle, always maintaining the balance.

"Don't threaten me, Oracle. Even I know not to test you." I pointed down at the nearest walkway. There was fresh blood trailing deeper in, and the sudden stench that followed instantly burned my nostrils. I needed to take a step back. "Is that the hellhound or the sewer?"

"Doesn't matter," said St. Claire, producing a short length of rope from under his jacket. "We're going down."

St. Claire attached his rope to a broken metal rod jutting out of the hole that had bent in a perfect sideways U. It supported his weight as he rappelled down.

"Fucking Oracle," I said under my breath, when he was out of earshot. I closed my eyes and focused on the only positive that came to mind. I couldn't kill the hellhound but I could still beat the shit out of it, which would be therapeutic. I hated the bastards with a passion. When I opened my eyes, St. Claire was looking up at me from the walkway, shaking the rope, offering it to me. I smiled before I jumped down to join him.

* * * * * * *

SERVICE LIGHTS GLOWED FAINTLY OVERHEAD along the walls, providing enough light that we didn't need our own light source. It was dimly lit tunnel after dimly lit tunnel, and it smelled like blood, shit, and piss.

"It isn't even down here, you fool," I said quietly.

"We both heard the screaming," said St. Claire, looking down another tunnel, following the trail of blood. "This blood is fresh." He put two fingers to the blood-smeared wall, showed them to me. "See?"

"I know fresh blood when I see it. I'm saying the beast is gone."

St. Claire shook his head. "No. The Oracle—"

I held up a hand to silence him.

"I'm telling you, the Oracle—"

I covered his mouth with my hand then and he stopped, trying to hear what I heard. It came again. The banging of something against metal. I put one finger to my lips and St. Claire nodded his head in understanding. I released him and we moved slowly, in silence. The banging came again, this time much louder, as if from all around us.

I looked around, studying our surroundings. Nothing was immediately visible, yet the sound seemed to be coming from everywhere—from all around us. St. Claire tapped my shoulder before pointing my attention up, above us. Weaving around the entire ceiling and branching off into the whole sewer system: metal pipes. "I was about to figure it out," I whispered.

"I don't doubt it," he whispered with a little smile. I continued to walk on. "Where are you going?"

"To find the damn thing before it finds us!" I shouted over my shoulder. The banging was getting louder and louder. I couldn't figure out if we were getting closer to the source or if it was getting closer to us.

* * * * * * *

IT TOOK US A FEW MINUTES TO UNDERSTAND what the hellhound was doing. In my excitement to fight without Anthony Monroe's incessant nagging, I didn't realize the beast wasn't running to us. It was running away. "Fucking cowardly creature," I spat when St. Claire pointed it out.

We were running, trying to keep up with a supernatural beast known for its vicious nature. Most would call what we were doing a suicide mission. Its howl echoed through the tunnels from ahead as someone else screamed. "Shit," said St. Claire. "It isn't running from us. It's chasing the survivors."

We were sprinting now, headed down the tunnel the scream had come from. We slowed as the tunnel ended, looking back and forth, side to side, as we progressed.

"*No*," a voice whispered from the shadows. "*No. Morirás. Morirás.*"

"What?" I asked the darkness.

St. Claire was rubbing his neck, thinking. "It's Spanish," he mumbled. "You forget where we are."

"Well, what did he say?"

"I don't know."

"You'll die," the man whispered as he stepped out from behind some vertical pipes. He had wedged himself between them and the wall of the tunnel. He was soaked in blood from head to toe, his eyes hollow as he stared past us. He twitched slightly, looking in the direction we were heading. "You'll die," he repeated.

"You'll die," he continued. "You'll die. You'll die." St. Claire and I could only watch as trauma broke him. The man shook his head in his hands, smearing the blood across his face. He kept repeating it, over and over. "You'll die."

"Well," I said as I looked at St. Claire, "he clearly speaks some English." I grabbed the man by the collar of his shirt and pulled him close. St. Claire tried to stop me but I shoved him back. "Where is it?"

"You'll die."

I shook the man once. "Where did it go?"

"You'll—"

"Hey!" I shook him again. "Look at me, you fucking pathetic man. You'll die if you don't tell us where it went."

He pointed down the tunnel, where it branched into three directions. "*Ve a la izquierda.*"

"I know that word," St. Claire cut in, looking down the tunnel. "He said go left."

"*¿Qué era?*" the man asked neither of us specifically. "*¿Un Chupacabra?*"

I ignored the man, no longer interested in anything he had to say. Tossing him aside, I made my way down the tunnel. St. Claire called for me to wait as he told the man to go out the way we came in. "Follow the blood all the way back," he told the man slowly, hoping he understood. "There's a rope."

The hellhound had stopped making a commotion midway through our conversation, meaning it was either gone or hunting its next meal. I turned the corner, to the left like the man had said, and I was suddenly and swiftly lifted from the ground, thrown into the air by something massive. I slammed into the wall on the opposite side of the tunnel, across the sewage below. The rubble fell on my head from where I smashed into the wall as I groaned, struggling to get on my hands and knees. "That doesn't count," I muttered as my spine snapped back into place. "I wasn't ready."

The hellhound growled as I shoved myself up to my feet. Its glowing red eyes were visible in the darkness, clearly locked onto me. I returned the creature's rageful gaze with a wicked grin across my face. "Finally!" I shouted, excited to let loose.

Shotgun shells suddenly pelted the bloodhounds' blood-red fur as St. Claire joined us, stepping into the sewer section. "You can't kill it, Lordal!" he reminded me.

"I haven't even touched it." I spat while I stumbled to my feet, brushing the rubble off. My spine was now fully healed, fused back together by demonic power.

The hellhound lowered itself to the ground, stalking a path toward St. Claire. He calmly eased into his steps backwards as he reloaded his shotgun.

I cracked my neck as I walked to the edge of the sewage between us. The beast had separated us immediately. It wasn't some dull, dim-witted creature. It demonstrated its intelligence with every move. "Hey!" I shouted, my voice deep and commanding. "I'm not done with you!"

The hellhound immediately curled itself back, turning toward me. It slicked itself forward and stopped along the edge of the sewage. It sat calmly across from me. It didn't move, just stared at me silently with its glowing red eyes.

"Lordal, you can't—" St. Claire tried to say, but the hellhound snapped its head back at him, snarling. He aimed his shotgun at the creature but didn't say another word.

The beast nodded in satisfaction before turning back to me. It opened its mouth then, speaking in a voice that sounded like static. "Lordal. We have found you."

I moved along the sewage, looking for a way to cross. The beast's gaze followed me but it remained where it sat. "That's funny. I thought we found you."

"Lordal—" St. Claire tried again, though the hellhound quickly turned to silence him.

"Do not speak again, Oracle," it warned. "Or I will tear your throat out, like I did your previous host. Not even your worthless gift can protect you from me. Now be silent."

St. Claire fired at the creature's face, catching it by surprise. The hellhound shook its head, slightly dazed by the impact. It snarled as his next shot knocked it off balance.

I took the opportunity to leap over the sewage while it was distracted, using a hanging pipe from the demon's earlier commotion to swing back to the other side. I slammed into the hellhound from above, knocking it back and cratering it into the wall. The creature recovered quickly and launched forward, tackling me before I could get back to my feet. Tumbling with the creature, I tore into its fur with my bare hands, our roars both deafening as we fell backwards into the sewage.

ANTHONY

I SHOUTED AS I FELL FROM THE SKY, ESCAPING THE blue fog once again. The sensation of falling was short as the ground rushed up to meet me. I crashed into planks of wood, splinters digging into my skin as I did.

"Where the hell am I now?" I said aloud to myself as I rubbed the back of my head and got back to my feet. Wincing from the pain in my body, I had to remind myself that this wasn't real. That this was still one of the Oracle's tricks. It was all just another illusion of events that was unfolding in my mind. I needed a moment to calm down, to process what was happening, but a quick look around only rattled me further. I knew exactly where I was, only it wasn't the way I had last seen Santa Monica Pier.

Now, instead of a small amusement park and droves of people enjoying the California sunshine, the Pier was empty and almost completely destroyed. Dead. It was all that came to mind. Holes littered the pier's wooden planks, and flames were still burning among the scrapheaps that had once brought joy to so many people. Below, fires burned piles of floating trash and debris in the polluted ocean. It was clear from what remained of the place that this happened recently.

"Joseph?" I called out to the ruins.

Lordal?

Nothing. It was odd. I didn't feel Lordal's presence as I once had. I hadn't realized how accustomed I'd grown to hearing his voice. I closed my eyes, reached out for his flame deep within, but there was nothing there. I was powerless and alone.

The rustle of wings drew my attention to the orange and gray sky. It looked like fires had been burning around the area for days, polluting the air with ash. The sun was barely visible through it all. I looked on, hoping to catch a glimpse of whatever was flying above me. Three dots appeared in the sky and as they grew closer, their polished skin and wings became clearer. For some reason, seeing them... I knew they couldn't be angels. I realized then where the Oracle had sent me. This was the war. This was Hell on Earth.

The three dots came down quickly but elegantly, revealing themselves to be three women. I had never seen such beautiful women before in my entire life. They were the spitting image of beauty in the modern world, but they were certainly not angels — or even fallen angels, like Lucifer. I could see now that their wings were scaled, not feathered. They were demons.

I quickly scanned the area, sprinting over to what remained of one of the Pier's concession stands. I recognized what was left of the branding as I hid behind it. I used to stop by for snacks when I'd come here, before Lordal had changed everything about my life. I ducked down as the three demons landed softly, sending dust and ash flying as their wings flapped once more before coming to a rest. I peeked over the stand to get a better look, still unsure if I existed in this space and time or if I was like a ghost, freely able to walk around as an unseen observer. I wasn't going to test my theories with these three.

It was truly upsetting just how beautiful these demons were. They looked as if they were sculpted of marble by artists from ancient periods. One was sculpted of a light pink color, with straight red hair that reached down to the small of her back, with hazel eyes. The one made of pure white marble had luscious black curls, her gray eyes looking at what remained of the Pier. The last was sculpted from a beautiful black marble, with messy blonde hair and emerald-green eyes. They all stood well over six feet tall and wore armor I had never seen before. They were all clearly warriors. They had probably just burned this place down.

They only waited for a moment before a ring of fire began to form farther down the Pier, erupting toward the sky as it reached completion. Then a hand emerged from the flames, separating the fire to reveal an all-too-familiar face. The face of Orm Gon—who I now knew to be my own personal demon, Lordal—emerged. The demon stepped out of the circle and the wind carried the flames away as the magic of the hellfire was broken.

"What news do you bring me, Furies?"

I heard him speak but his voice also echoed in my own head, as if he was still within me.

"Where have you been?"

He sounded nothing like the Lordal I knew. His familiar rage was replaced with regality, an assertiveness. He was jacked, with muscles I didn't even know existed. His dreads were tied back in a knot. He wore armor that seemed to meld with his skin, made of some strange black metal coated with his flames.

The Furies bowed before him, extending their arms toward him. "Forgive us, Lord," said the pink one. "The resistance is more resourceful than expected. The new hunters continue to aid them."

I sank back behind the counter as I remembered what the Oracle told me: "You must see the truth. This is his destiny, so it will be yours."

Lordal wasn't serving the King of Hell here. He was the King of Hell—or rather, he was going to be. I prayed that this was only a possibility. That the Oracle could somehow stop this from happening.

"I do not accept failure, Furies.

You know this, yet return empty-handed?"

Lordal stepped forward, gesturing for them to stand.

"Forgive us, Lord," said the one made of pure white. "His knowledge of your powers and forces proves vaster than we expected."

"We will bring them to their knees," said the one made of beautiful black marble. She stepped forward, bowing deeply. The others followed her lead. "We will never fail you, our Lord. Our savior from the Devil himself."

Lordal appeared satisfied by their response. He nodded confidently, then turned to walk down the Pier. The Furies followed closely as he continued to address them.

"Come, then.

We're not done reshaping this world.

My world."

The wind picked up, suddenly roaring and tearing apart the Pier piece by piece. The wooden planks and crumbled ruins of what remained in this nightmare of a world were ripped away, blown into an infinite black void. I was left floating again, covering my face from the vanishing debris. I lowered my arms slowly, staring out into the darkness. There was no point in showing me any of this if it couldn't be changed. There had to be a way to stop it, otherwise the whole world was already lost. It was only a matter of time.

With nothing to do but think, the big question finally hit me. Where was I in that future? What had happened to me? And where was the Devil? Had Lordal killed him? Lordal was supposed to stop Hell on Earth, wasn't he? If Lucifer had died, why was Lordal…

"What the hell is going on?" I said to no one in particular as I shook my head in misery. These visions, or whatever they were, only left me with more questions. Were we trying to stop this or was the Oracle showing me what we were preparing for? None of it made any sense.

Suddenly, a low boom erupted in the void, shaking me to my core. "Now you've seen the future we must change," the Oracle's voice surrounded me. Then, more hastily, he added, "You're needed back on Earth, Anthony Monroe."

I felt myself lurch forward as the world flipped.

LORDAL

"GET OUT OF HERE!" I SHOUTED AS THE BEAST tackled me back into the sewage. It entered my lungs and the filth nearly drowned me.

The hellhound was fierce. I had only faced one other this strong in my lifetime, although that was a long time ago and I was far weaker then. We struggled in the sewage, locked in combat. It thrashed about like a frenzied animal, snapping at me with its teeth, slashing at me with its claws. Every cut was deeper than the next. Our blood wasn't even visible in the filthy sewage we fought in.

"Get out of there, man!" I could hear St. Claire shouting from above. "Let's go!"

I felt myself go weightless as I was flung out of the sewage then. I smashed into a wall, fell down into the rubble. My leg was broken and my arm was bent in an awkward position. My blood was already pooling around me.

"What the fuck are you thinking?" shouted St. Claire. "That thing is killing you!"

I rubbed my shoulder briefly before jamming it back into place with a mild grunt. I spit the blood out of my mouth before struggling up to my feet. My wounds were healing slower. My foe wasn't of this world. "Not if I kill it first," I said to St. Claire, just as the sewage exploded in front of me and the beast's fangs stabbed into my throat, sinking deep into my neck. I could hear St. Claire firing off shells from his shotgun as the beast yanked me back down into the muck. It kept an iron grip around my throat as I struggled. I clenched my fists until they were glowing like hot steel, then I slammed my palms on to the beast's face, fusing its flesh to its bones. The hellhound released me after a few swings and I sloshed my way back out of the sewage.

"Behind you!" shouted St. Claire as I hoisted myself back up onto the walkway.

The hellhound exploded out of the sewage again in a rage, its one good eye locked onto me. I turned to face it, waving it on with a smile as I released flames from my hands. The creature lunged forward, my flaming fists connecting with its jaw as it snapped at me. It let out a yelp as its neck snapped from the impact, falling dead into the shit with a massive splash. I took a moment to catch my breath before I got to my feet, stumbling forward before I fell to my knees in the filth.

"That wasn't so—" I screamed as I gripped the sides of my head. The all-too familiar feeling surged through me as my mind was torn in two. It could only mean one thing: the boy. I cried out as my injuries began to slow their healing, my power once again bound by Lucifer's curse. My breaths grew short as I was suddenly dying, my injuries too severe for me to survive if they healed this slowly. It took all my effort to heal the vessel, stitching every muscle and tissue back together with my power before his return. Finally, I struggled to my feet once more, but my strength escaped me. I fell back into the filth, too exhausted from the healing process.

ANTHONY

I SAILED THROUGH THE BLUE FOG UNTIL MY HEAD exploded out of water and the stench of sewage filled my nose — it was sewage. I was desperate for fresh air as I gasped in the smell of shit. I was too angry to vomit. I could feel my blood boiling. I could feel Lordal, though only slightly, but I knew I was back.

"What the fuck is this?" I shouted.

"Anthony! Over here!" I heard Joseph from above me. "Come on! Hurry!"

"Why am I covered in crap, man?" I asked as I made my way to the Oracle. "And why—"

I stopped when I bumped into a hairy mass in the sewage with me. I didn't register what it was until I noticed its one eye dimming. It was a hellhound — the remains of one, at least. I flinched back instinctively, repulsed by the sight of the body.

"Hurry!" said Joseph, snapping his fingers to demand my attention.

My hands ran over the beast's wet fur as I attempted to maneuver around its massive corpse. I had plenty of questions that needed answers, but what killed this hellhound wasn't one of them. I stumbled through the sewage until arms appeared from above and hoisted me up. Joseph set me down against a wall, under a flickering green-tinted tunnel light. Before I could thank him, I suddenly felt all the wounds from Lordal's fight burn as they continued to heal.

"What happened? Where was I?" I asked, looking up at Joseph, who seemed distracted by something down the tunnel we were in. "Joseph!" I snapped. "What the fuck did you do to me?"

Joseph shook his head, rubbing his temples, clearly exhausted. "You both ask so many questions," he started, turning back to me and crouching down. "Look, you were shown whatever it is the Oracle wanted you to see. I have no idea what happened to you. Now," he continued, looking back over his shoulder, "we should really get out of here."

"What's the rush? Wasn't the hellhound the whole reason we're here?"

Joseph nodded, getting up and scanning the floor. He pointed a few feet away at something and reached down to pick up his shotgun. He quickly began to fiddle with it, reloading it as he walked back over to me. The Oracle was clearly communicating with him. He looked up, a blank expression on his face. "None of this would be happening," he said with a sigh, "if Lordal had just listened to me."

"What's wrong?" I asked, pushing myself back against the wall to slide up to my feet.

"None of the workers survived in my vision."

"So?"

"There's still one survivor. I sent him back the way we came in."

"So... What?" My injuries were fully healed now. I could stand comfortably. "We changed the future?"

Then a howl echoed down the tunnel, followed by the terrified screams of a man. We both turned, staring deep into the darkness, as something flew across the tunnel with immense force.

"No," said Joseph quietly, as a massive shadow leaped out of the darkness, splashing down into the sewage I was just pulled out of. Its eyes were glowing red hot, the beast clearly enraged. It snapped its jaws, snapping down on the man it brought with it, his body dangling from its mouth. His dying eyes stared at us. Joseph shook his head as he looked from me to the beast, raising his shotgun. "We can't change the future, Anthony."

"So, what do we do now then, wise guy?" I asked, backing up slowly as the hellhound advanced forward one step at a time. It growled deeply, lowering its head to sniff the corpse of its fallen kin. It lurched its head upward, howling in its grief. I covered my ears as the sound echoed through the tunnel.

Joseph took the opportunity to quickly pull a small needle-shaped device from one of his many jacket pockets. We slowly rounded a corner, our eyes locked with the beast's.

"We aren't going to fight?" I asked quietly.

"I'm pretty sure Lordal is spent, man," said Joseph, tossing the device to me. "You think you can take it on? Try stabbing it with this."

"What am I supposed to do with this?" I asked, examining the device he tossed into my hands. It was some sort of thick needle made of plated metal, with a blinking green light on the other end. It seemed to be some sort of tracking device. Another howl from back the way we'd come brought me back to our current predicament. "We're not getting far if we try to outrun this thing," I said as I looked around the tunnels for a way out. "Where are we even?"

"Not really the most important thing right now, Anthony," said Joseph, turning another corner. The hellhound wasn't far behind, rounding the last corner as we went around this one. "Clearly."

The beast sprang forward, pivoting around the corner and lunging towards us. Joseph fired his shotgun only once before the hellhound swooped down, chomping on the barrel and tossing him aside. He slammed into the wall across the sewage on the opposite walkway, crumbling to the floor. I looked down at the unfamiliar device in my hand as the hellhound locked its eyes on me. I stepped back slowly. What the fuck was I supposed to do now? I had just woken up from two nightmares to find myself in a third.

Run.

Lordal's voice echoed in my mind, giving me a sudden sense of direction. I turned, sprinting as fast as I could down the narrow path. The hellhound gave chase, launching after me at a much faster pace. It passed me immediately and as I slowed to a stop it quickly turned, slamming me to the ground with a flick of its tail. I hit the ground hard, losing the air in my lungs from the impact. My vision was spotty as I tried to push myself off the ground. The beast slammed into me and instinctively I tried to push it off, unintentionally forcing the tracking device deep into its skin. It growled, then a searing pain shot through my arm. I lurched back, kicking out at the creature with my feet as I fell back. Looking down, my eyes grew wide at the sight of what had happened to my arm.

It was gone.

"That's funny," I heard Joseph say to himself as he began picking himself up across the way. "That was one of my original ideas."

My ears began to ring as I screamed, unable to hear even Lordal in my head as I watched blood spray from the wound. My mind was now haunted by the sight of my own bones and muscles cut clean. The hellhound had chomped off my arm. Already, I felt like it was on fire.

Then I remembered that I didn't die in the forest. I doubted I would die from this. It still hurt like hell though, and I couldn't get my grip back on reality. It was all too surreal.

Breathe.

Lordal's voice resonated inside me, guiding me through the process of channeling his power from deep within.

Focus.

The flame is in you. It can heal you.

Concentrate on the flame.

I breathed deep, trying to focus on his voice and the flame. It was difficult with the fatigue Lordal's fight had already caused to my body.

I groaned suddenly as I felt myself being lifted up, my feet dragging along the ground until I finally got them moving on their own. I looked over to my side to see Joseph helping me through the tunnels. Suddenly, he released me again before a flash of light went off. I stumbled sideways before he caught me.

My vision spotted as I tried to focus on Lordal's words. I could do this. I could heal myself. I just needed to concentrate, but I was bleeding out. The heat coursed through my body, pumped through my veins. My vision blurred as flames began to erupt off of me, running over my eyes. Joseph jumped back in terror, letting me go as the flames wrapped around my shoulder, burning down my arm. I roared, dropping to the ground as embers began to spiral out of my injury. The wound began to seal, growing a new limb with every new layer of flame. I felt the heat of the fire, what it truly meant to burn. The rapid healing process was painful but necessary, a downside to this eternal curse. The flames died then and I sighed in relief. The pain faded and my mind was suddenly clear. I pushed myself to my feet, keeping low as I gathered my surroundings, still fatigued from the whole experience. I looked down at my new arm, closing and opening my new hand a few times. It was so fascinating that I forgot the danger I was in as the light of the fire died from my body. My breathing calmed as the heat dissipated from my veins.

"Joseph?" I finally whispered into the dark.

"Over here," I heard as a hand touched my shoulder, guiding me backwards into the shadows. Joseph pulled me back against the wall in a corner. Most of the lights in our tunnel had been destroyed by the rampage of the second hellhound. He grabbed my hand, guiding me along the wall until I felt him move it onto a solid metal bar. Joseph leaned close as another howl echoed throughout the tunnels, followed by the splashing of massive paws in the sewage. The hellhound had our scent.

"Up," said Joseph, and I could just barely make out his hand in front of my face. He was pointing upwards, somewhere in the dark. When I didn't move, he said, "It's a ladder, Anthony. Go."

I shook my head, feeling stupid for hesitating. I began to feel above and sure enough, more rungs extended overhead. The only question I had was where it led—I didn't see any light above—but I knew my constant questions annoyed the Oracle. I climbed the ladder, higher and higher into the darkness, until I reached a solid ceiling. I felt around, searching in the dark as the sounds of the hellhound grew closer. My hand fell over something, a handle of some sort. I tugged and it creaked. I calmed myself once more, focusing on the flame inside me. It wasn't just for healing, it was Lordal's power. By focusing on it, I could tap into it whenever I needed. I smiled in the dark as I realized how much control I now had. It seemed that using his power didn't require a full transition of our minds, and that I could use it even when he wasn't willing to fight for me. I focused on the strength of the flame, turning the handle with a loud creak. I shoved upward with my shoulder, forcing the hatch open. It swung open with ease, banging on the ground above. I scrambled out of the tunnel, sprawling out onto the floor of the room I was now in.

I thought Joseph was right behind me but I heard one final shotgun blast below, then a roar in the tunnels as a flash blinked out. Moments later, Joseph pulled himself up into the room, kicking the hatch shut behind him. He fell next to me, spreading out on the floor as well. We caught our breath in silence, surrounded by the smell of shit that covered us.

"What... What the fuck?" I whispered in awe after a few minutes. "I lost my goddamn arm, then..." I waved my hands in the air above me. "It was back. But, like, with fire."

"Yeah, what the hell was that?" said Joseph, stifling a laugh.

"What's so funny? I nearly died."

"You were tweaking hard, man. Running around with one arm, flailing about," he said, laughing. "And then you caught on fire out of fucking nowhere."

"Grew my whole fucking arm back, dude!"

We both laughed for a moment. We stayed there, laying in the darkness, covered in shit, laughing into the empty void around us. Finally, Joseph got on his feet first and explored the room. "There's a door over here," he told me.

I made my way towards Joseph's voice, searching in the dark with a ball of fire formed in my hand. We needed to get out of here before the hellhound decided it wanted a rematch.

"Can you get it open?" I asked as I came up beside him. It was a big metal sliding door, a giant lock and chain keeping it secure. I pointed down at it. "I'm guessing not."

Joseph pointed at the ball of fire I held in my hand.

"Oh, right," I mumbled. "Duh."

I held the flame close to the lock until it melted and the chain clanked onto the ground. Joseph pulled the chain from the door, tossing it aside. We grabbed the bars on the door, sliding it open only to reveal another dark tunnel. There was something different about this one though. It wasn't a part of the sewer system.

"You feel that?" Joseph asked, sticking his head out the door. I shook my head. "It's a breeze. Fresh air. This tunnel is connected to the surface. Look down there." He pointed to the ground. "Tracks."

I tossed a small fireball into the tunnel, revealing a series of tracks laying across the ground. I waved my hand before the ball touched the ground, extinguishing it. I was getting so used to the power without Lordal taking control that I almost forgot he was even there. I wondered if he could feel that—if he was okay with it.

"Where do you think they lead?" I asked, following Joseph as he hopped down to the tracks.

The gravel shifted beneath our feet as we touched down, scattering rocks across the rails. He looked back and forth, trying to determine which way to go. "My guess," he started, "is that we're in an older section of the Mexico City subway system. If we follow this tunnel, we should end up at one of the operating platforms."

Joseph's expression was grim in the dim light as he led the way. We turned back when a howl echoed from below, both of us waiting to hear a hellhound chasing us. For a moment, I thought I heard the scratching of claws followed by the splashing of sewage, but it all faded away. Joseph and I both exhaled quietly before we resumed our walk, continuing down the tunnel side by side.

* * * * * * *

WE WALKED IN SILENCE FOR HALF AN HOUR UNTIL we reached the first platform. A few howls echoed from various cracks and openings that led below, letting us know the hellhound was still running around in the sewer system. It wasn't until we were maybe forty yards from the platform ahead that I finally broke the silence. "You know what that was." It wasn't a question. It was a statement.

"Yeah." Joseph kept looking forward. "I know what it was."

"No, not the hellhound." I stopped walking, staring at him as he continued to walk away. "The visions. What were they?"

"A warning," he said without slowing down. "And a way of understanding. The past is the foundation for the present, and the present guides us into the future. The future is uncertain until we arrive upon it."

"Back down there, you said we can't change the future. You knew it wasn't over because there was still a survivor."

Joseph stopped then, turning halfway to face me from his side. "Don't misunderstand. There are always multiple possibilities of how, but it will come to be."

"So, the future is always what you see, but has different ways of playing out?" I asked, trying to wrap my head around what this meant for me—for what I saw.

He nodded his head, turning back toward the platform. "Now you're starting to get it."

Joseph strolled forward casually with his hands tucked in his jacket pockets. I stared at him for a moment, annoyed that I was left with more questions than I started with. Did I have a bigger purpose than I could see right now? I shook my head. So much power, and so many people seeking to control it, direct it, or destroy it. Was Lordal just a weapon to everyone? Was this the life he was left with?

"Okay," I started as I caught up to Joseph. The thought occurred to me from our conversion before. "There's something else that's been bothering me. You said mankind was unprepared for an attack from Hell. That it had forgotten the ways of magic or something."

"Something like that, sure."

"Before your shadow man—"

Phantom figure.

"Luka," said Joseph.

"Before I was brought to you," I finished, annoyed with them both. "There was—" I had no desire to relive the redwood forest. I kept it simple and said, "There was a man, kept calling himself a hunter. Lordal and I fought him. He said it was his mission to kill me."

That's putting it nicely.

Joseph clicked his tongue as we made it to the platform. He used the small ladder built into the side to get up. "Demon hunters," he said as he climbed. "Yes, they exist. Naturally, people fear things they do not understand. Night creatures are one of those things."

"Night creatures?" I asked as I came up behind him. I remembered the term from somewhere… Then it came to me. Orm Gon, Hunter of the Night Creatures. Lucifer had said it.

"Any creature of supernatural descent," Joseph continued, extending a hand down to help me up. "The misunderstood. Night creatures aren't just hellhounds. Demons who were once men, for example. The people they possess. So on."

"How do you know so much about this stuff?" I brushed off some dirt as we looked around the platform. It was completely empty, save the trash that littered the place and old graffiti on the walls. This part of the subway was clearly retired long ago.

"I was a hunter," said Joseph, making his way to the staircase that led up to the surface. "Come on. We smell like shit."

I tried to piece more of my new world together as we made our way up the stairs. "If you're a hunter," I asked slowly, "why are you helping me?"

"I was a hunter. I've got bigger things going on upstairs now," he said, pointing at his head like he tended to do. "That hellhound was going to die before it killed Elizabeth. It just went and made things personal."

"You don't think the Oracle knew what was going to happen to her?"

"I need to believe it didn't. My eyes have been opened to a new reality, Anthony. One where a demon is meant to save the world from the Devil. Why would I hunt him down and become his enemy?"

"Because he's a monster, just like the rest," said a woman from the shadows behind us.

It felt like déjà vu—an arrow whizzed through the air, slamming into my chest as I turned around in my surprise. I managed to maintain my footing this time though, instead of falling back. I screamed in agony while I pulled at the projectile lodged in my chest with both hands. "FUCK!" I shouted.

"Here," said Joseph, reaching for the arrow. "Let—" He stopped short as another arrow whizzed between us, vanishing into the dark.

"Step away from the demon!" we heard. Joseph turned to face the woman stepping from the shadows with a bow aimed at his chest. She wore white and black combat robes, her bow and arrows matching the gear. Blonde hair toppled over her hooded face and she brushed it out of the way. "My battle is not with you."

"I'm okay, man," I lied with a smile.

"Don't do anything stupid, demon," said the woman. "Or we may just discover how many lives you really have."

"Who are you?" shouted Joseph.

The throbbing in my head worsened. Like the last hunter that attacked me, the woman's arrowheads were coated with poison. The only difference this time was that Lordal wasn't in any condition to help me. I collapsed to my knees, sweating, watching my veins turn black as the toxin worked its way through my body. I looked up at the lady, staring at her with absolute rage. "What the hell, lady?" I shouted at her.

Rather than answering our questions, she moved forward and released her next arrow. It pierced my throat and my eyes widened in shock. I gurgled as blood began to fill my lungs and I gripped the arrow in horror. I turned to Joseph who stared back, eyes also wide in shock. I fell backwards, rolling down the stairs and off the platform. I coughed up blood as I crashed onto the tracks.

"Anthony!" I heard Joseph. He was suddenly at my side, trying to get me back on my feet. "You need to get up! We need to get out of here! Get up! Get up, man!"

He repeated it over and over, attempting to drag me off the tracks. That's when I began to feel it. The ground started trembling beneath us. Stones leapt from the ground as lights flooded the tunnel. I toppled my head towards them.

Barreling along the tracks towards us was a train. The conductor must have seen us there on the ground because the horn was blaring. I thought my ears had been ringing from the blood loss. I closed my eyes, preparing to be splattered across the tunnel.

I can save us.

Give me control.

Now, boy.

I faded into the back of my mind. The last thing I felt was my blood beginning to boil as an eerie howl blended in with the sound of the oncoming train's horn.

LORDAL

MY EYES SNAPPED OPEN AS FLAMES ROARED OVER my skin. I yanked the arrow out of my throat, healing instantly, then took St. Claire under my arm and jumped back onto the platform in an effortless leap. The train barreled past just as we landed on the ground.

"You're welcome." I grunted as I threw the Oracle to the ground, feeling the poison from the arrow in my chest. I yanked it out before I fell to my knees. I was still weak but the boy wasn't ready to handle this himself.

Suddenly, from behind, a blade pressed against my throat, sliding across just as quickly as it appeared. I choked as I fell forward, wrapping my hands around my throat.

"Pathetic," said a voice from behind.

I rolled over to face my attacker; hands now covered in blood as they held my neck. She was indeed a huntress, wearing the robes of hunters I had faced in many of my lifetimes. How the hunter clans were finding me so easily was beginning to trouble me, but there wasn't time to give it any thought.

Flames roared from my hands, burning into my slit throat. I screamed in rage as it healed. My screams turned to gurgles, then

I spat out blood and chuckled. Pushing myself up from the dirt, I cracked my stiff neck before I said, "I'm not dead yet."

I roared as flames leapt from my hands and I lunged forward, tackling her past Joseph back onto the tracks. I slammed her into the ground, pinning her down before she could reach for her sword. St. Claire and I both cursed under our breath when we heard a howl in the tunnels. I turned toward the sound. Walking along the tracks toward us, bringing the stench of the sewer with it, was the surviving hellhound. I slammed the Huntress into the ground again without breaking eye contact with the beast. It lowered, crouching as it approached, growling. I tossed the unconscious Huntress back onto the platform with St. Claire. I waved my hand at the hellhound, inviting it to its bloody death.

"Lordal!" shouted St. Claire.

"What?" I shouted, stepping towards the beast.

"We need it alive!"

"Fine." I grunted, spitting the last of the blood out of my mouth. I waved my hand at the hellhound. "Come and get it."

The beast sprung from the ground, descending on me. I dodged to the side, wrapping my arms around its neck as it passed. Using its momentum, I slammed it face-first into the ground. Dirt exploded around us as it smashed through the tracks. I stumbled back as the hound raised its head from the debris, shaking its head back and forth. It turned to me, barking loudly. Fire burst from my hands as I launched flames through the air toward the monster. The fire exploded against its fur but it seemed to have no effect. It snapped its jaws down on my arm, crunching down and drawing blood. I cried out, exploding my entire arm in flames. It released its grip, leaping back as the fire healed my wound. I groaned as I pulled one of its teeth out of my arm.

"Oracle!" I shouted, wobbling from my exhaustion. "If you don't help, I'm killing this thing." The hound turned toward me again and I braced myself for the next attack. "St. Claire!" I shouted again as I held my fists up. Flames leapt from them, encircling them in the power of hellfire.

"Just give it a minute!" I heard him shout back. The hound turned towards me again and I braced myself for the next attack.

"Oracle!" I shouted again, circling the beast on the tracks. "A little sooner would be nice!"

"Twelve seconds!"

"Until what!"

The tunnel was suddenly flooded with light and I shielded my eyes against another oncoming train. Its horn blared as it barreled into the tunnel. I sprinted to the platform, leaping up and taking Joseph's hand. He helped me over the edge as the hellhound sprang forward. It slammed into the train with its full force, derailing it off the tracks.

The train flew through the station, separating us all. I lost sight of the others before I was knocked back by debris.

* * * * * * *

I LAID IN THE MESS FOR A MOMENT, PRAYING something would just kill me so I could finally catch my breath, but I knew better than to hope for such mercy. Groaning, I pushed myself back up onto my feet. Dust, dirt, and flames filled the air. The sound of cracking rock echoed throughout the structure. I noticed immediately that the hellhound was gone, and so was the Huntress. And a massive derailed train now rested in the middle of the station, keeping the whole place from coming down for a few more moments.

"St. Claire?" I shouted, stumbling to the side as I held my hands against my ears to stop the ringing. "Oracle? Answer me!"

I heard someone approaching behind me and I turned to see the bloodied face of Joseph St. Claire. He held up a thumbs-up before collapsing into the rubble.

"What the hell happened?" I asked.

St. Claire looked up at me as he rubbed the side of his head. He was bleeding from a wound on his forehead. "The hellhound derailed the train," he told me. "Thought that was obvious."

"Come on," I started, extending my hand down to help him up. "You know, you're shit at seeing the future."

"Yeah, yeah," said St. Claire with a chuckle as he got on his feet. "Don't make me laugh. It hurts."

"We need to go before the hellhound returns," I told him. "I'm too weak to keep going like this."

"Really?" said St. Claire, wobbling on his feet. "I can keep going. I dare it to come back."

"You sound like the boy."

"Heroic?"

"Annoying."

St. Claire grabbed me by the arm as I started for the stairs, pointing at the train cars in the middle of all the mess. "What about the passengers?"

"What about them?" I asked, looking back at where he was pointing. "Leave them."

We can't leave them.

They'll die before anyone finds them.

"We do not have time for this."

St. Claire now seemed accustomed to being left out of the conversations. He sat down on the stairs to catch his breath, fully aware that the boy was distracting me.

Lordal, we have the power to help people.

All we ever do is fight.

This is our chance to do something good.

"These people would sooner see us dead than be saved by us. Don't forget what I am, boy. How many lives I've lived. Humans hate the supernatural. They'll do anything to rid themselves of it."

They're not all like that.

Joseph changed.

"He's an exception." I shook my head, looking back at the collapsing station. "You don't understand."

Help them, Lordal.

LORDAL

Maybe one day they'll see you as more than a demon.

This is a chance at redemption.

"No," I said as I allowed the boy to take control. "You want to save them? Do it yourself."

ANTHONY

I WAS TOO WEAK TO GET THE DOORS OPEN ALONE. "Can you help me out?" I asked through gritted teeth, struggling to pry them open. I couldn't feel Lordal's flame, couldn't tap into his strength to assist me.

Joseph wasn't in great shape either but he joined me, finding a broken piece of metal and wedging it between the doors of the train. On the other side, the passengers watched in panic as we struggled to save them.

"I wasn't talking to you," I admitted to Joseph.

Me?

I glanced upwards. It might have looked like a prayer, like I was talking to God, though He clearly abandoned me as soon as Lordal entered my mind.

Why should I?

"You have all this power and you're too afraid to use it unless you have to. You're selfish, Lordal. That's why humanity hates you."

Do you think I asked for this?

To be undying for eight thousand years?

I will never find peace or happiness, boy.

Be grateful that you only have one life to lose.

You will never know this suffering.

"You pathetic fucking asshole," I nearly shouted, ignoring Joseph's reaction to my sudden profanity. "I hate you because you do all the wrong things, and never any good. All that power and eternal life wasted on someone so miserable. Think of all the things you could have done. How you could have changed the world. Ended so much suffering. Only you didn't, did you?"

Joseph and I paused as the hellhound roared somewhere in the mess. I looked back at the destroyed tunnel for a moment, returning to my efforts on the doors after confirming the hellhound wasn't right behind us.

"We need to get out of here," said Joseph, trying his best to help me. It was useless. We were getting nowhere. I sank to the floor, my head hung low. Joseph placed a hand on my shoulder. "Anthony…"

"Why me?" I looked up at him. "Why is this all happening to me? And the one time I want to do something right, I can't. Can your Oracle tell me that?"

I got to my feet, walking away as I did my best to connect with the demon inside me. To find a way to call upon his power. I had done it before. Why couldn't I do it now?

Lordal stopped talking but I could still feel his flame. I focused on the heat within me, calming down my breathing. He was wrong. I did know his suffering. I knew his pain. I'd seen it. I was living it. He and I were one now. I could use his abilities with or without his approval. When I was dying underneath the redwoods, I hadn't given up control to heal. When I lost my arm, it grew back without the demon emerging. It occurred to me that perhaps I didn't need to give Lordal control of my life. It was the will of the soul he was bonded with that controlled him. He was cursed, bound to his host, but it went both ways. I felt the heat flow through me, embracing me as I willingly embraced it. Steam rose from my skin as my hands began to glow. The power of Lordal was mine to control.

"Stand back," I told Joseph, placing my hands against the doors as the fire crackled inside my veins. My palms began to burn and soon the metal melted, forming holes for my hands to grip the doors. I grabbed my makeshift handles and yanked the doors free, tossing them back as people began to stream out of the train car. "Head towards the stairs!" I shouted as they thanked me and made their way through the debris. "Everybody out! Now! There isn't much time!"

I made sure everyone got out of the train before helping Joseph up to the surface. No one stayed behind to help us but it didn't matter. They were safe, and the demon's power had done some good. It was unclear if Lordal allowed me to take his power or if I took it myself, but I liked to think he decided to help. That he understood we were two sides of the same coin. That he changed.

"You did a good job, Anthony," said Joseph while we made our way up the stairs.

I nodded but said nothing as we reached the top. A loud rumbling noise came from below as we moved away from the station. We turned back briefly to see the structure come down. All around us, people were calling loved ones and embracing each other, grateful to have survived.

I did this. I was suddenly understanding it all now. This wasn't Lordal. This was me. Clarity hadn't struck him. It struck me. His sins were mine. His past was mine. His fear was mine. I was Lordal, just as much as he was Anthony Monroe. He didn't exist without me and I no longer existed without him.

Clarity is a beautiful thing.

Of course he understood. I was only beginning to. There hadn't been time to process anything.

Do you smell that?

I sniffed the air and smelled the familiar shitty scent of the hellhound underground, but there was something else. The Huntress. She was still alive, probably searching for us even now.

There still wasn't time to process anything, evidently.

I turned to Joseph, who had paused against the crumbling pillar outside the ruined station. "We need to go," I told him.

* * * * * * *

I TUCKED MYSELF BACK INTO THE ALLEYWAY, pulling the collar of Joseph's jacket back up around my face. I took the hood off, revealing my weary face.

The Huntress was nearby. I could smell her, faintly, though it was growing increasingly difficult. Her scent was fading in and out. "We need to get out of here," I said to Joseph, who had sat down on the ground and started meditating. "Joseph? Did you hear me?"

He held up a hand to shush me. "Just because you're deeply connected to your entity now does not mean you can disrespect me and mine."

"We need to leave, Joseph," I continued, crouching next to him. "The Huntress isn't far and the hellhound can still find us. I can't keep fighting. If I can't, there's no way you can."

After we left the station, we hurried a few blocks away to put some distance between ourselves and the scene. I'd pulled us off into this alleyway, only for Joseph to immediately sit down and enter some sort of meditative state. Which—and Lordal would agree—we didn't have time for. We were lucky that our misadventures were in an abandoned part of the city but the authorities had to be on their way. The destruction must have been heard—if not on the surface, then echoed throughout the subway system. No doubt the tunnel was blocked and trains were stopped. People would be looking for who was responsible, and I had openly used my powers. We needed to leave.

"I know," mumbled Joseph, nodding to himself, completely ignoring me. "I just— Hmm... Yes."

"Hey!" a voice shouted from the end of the alley. Suddenly, the scent of the Huntress was more present than ever. I turned to see her making her way towards us, still alive and well. Clearly, dropping a train station on this woman wasn't enough to stop her.

"We aren't done yet," she said as she began to sprint, wielding a staff by her side. I could see from where I stood that it had the same markings as all the weapons used against me under the redwoods, which meant fighting her would probably hurt about the same too.

"How does she mask her scent like that?" I asked no one in particular.

She's a professional.

Right, duh.

"Honestly, lady," I said, stepping forward and raising my hands. "Kindly fuck off."

I exhaled some heat, preparing to create a wall of fire to protect us—or at least buy us some time. I slammed my hands into the ground, creating a flaming barrier that rose up between us. She stopped short a few feet from my flames, already searching for a way around them. "You think this will stop me, demon?" she shouted.

I turned to Joseph, who was already back on his feet. "The Jeep, Joseph. Now. I'll distract her."

"Right." He nodded to me before sprinting off. "I'll be back."

I turned back to face the deadly woman. She had vanished from the other side.

"Lady!" I shouted over the roar of the fire. "I don't want to kill you! Just let me walk away."

"I can't do that."

My eyes followed the sound of her voice up a fire escape along the left side of the alley. I saw her just as she came at me, leaping over my flames with ease. She brought down the end of her staff, smashing it across my face as she landed gracefully in front of me. I wobbled back, regaining my balance as the heat numbed the pain from her blow. I rubbed the spot where she'd hit me, wiping away the blood. "What is your problem?" I asked as I conjured fireballs in my hands. "Just let us leave!"

I threw the fireballs down at her feet and she dodged out of the way as they exploded on the ground.

"You are possessed by a monster, an unearthly creation that must be destroyed." She slammed her staff on the ground. "God did not make you in His image, therefore you are impure. Thus, you cannot be allowed to go on in this world."

"That's why you hunt demons?" I said sarcastically, circling away from her. "Honestly, lady, it sounds like you're in some sort of psycho cult."

"I simply seek to end your suffering." She collapsed her staff suddenly, shrinking it down with a flick of her wrist. It became a small rectangular box with an unnatural shimmer to it. The box was much smaller than made sense for the size of what her staff had been. She slipped it into a pocket in her robes and pulled out another shimmering object, with the same unnatural presence. She held it between her hands, whispering to the strange object softly. The metal began to seep through her fingers, covering them as it transformed into a liquid before solidifying around her hands. She looked at me then and said, "Surely, you understand that I'm trying to help you."

"What're you doing, lady?" I asked, taking a step back.

You should have stopped her, instead of gawking.

"You cannot tell me that the demon inside you doesn't know great pain. Life after life, death after death. Eternal suffering. You helped those people earlier, boy." She brought her metal fists together, causing white sparks to crackle off them as she formed a unique battle stance. "You were pure until this evil tainted you. I shall be the one to rip this evil from you."

Run.

That's not going to sting like the generator in the woods.

"Wait, what?" I said in a panic, backing away from the Huntress. "What do you mean? What the fuck do you mean?"

The Huntress raised her hands and white lightning shot from her palms. I turned to run, only to be struck in the side within seconds. I was sent flying through the brick wall of the warehouse beside us. I crashed into another wall, falling to the ground where I laid in agony, half dead from the pain in my side. All around me were wooden crates, some scattered on the floor and most stored neatly on racks. I pushed my way out from under the debris, blood dripping from where I was hit. I looked down at my side, the pain still incredible despite my new demonic abilities. Hundreds of tiny sparks were jumping around my scorched flesh where I was struck.

"Why the fuck won't it stop burning?" I cried out as I cursed louder.

Lightning of the Acaries.

That's a big spell for anyone to carry.

"Did you just say spell?" I asked through gritted teeth. The pain was like nothing I had ever experienced, and I had been killed a few times. "Like, witches and wizards?"

Yes, if they want to call themselves something so mundane.

This woman isn't a witch.

She's a hunter.

I struggled to my feet, then looked around for an exit. I needed to get to Joseph. We needed to get the hell out of here.

You should have cooked her.

"Please just tell me about spells," I said, ignoring his critique. Holding my aching side, I stumbled farther into the warehouse. He may have been right but I only wanted to stall the woman, not kill her. There was also no way I was getting hit by another Lightning of the Acaries spell though. That shit fucking hurt, and it didn't seem to be healing either.

Hunters often carry spells or enchantments, as you saw.

You really should have stopped her from activating it.

"Not the time, Lordal," I said as I ducked through a door into a larger section of the warehouse. Light filtered down from skylights in the ceiling high above. Joseph had to be nearby by now. I just needed to survive long enough to escape. "Tell me more about them. I'm sick and tired of not knowing anything."

Metal is a popular choice to store magic.

It's easy to activate with a simple heat incantation.

Though you can use other activators.

In Ancient Egypt, they used wands and amulets.

"Like witches and wizards," I whispered as I stumbled through the warehouse, waiting for any sign of Joseph. "Lordal, focus. Am I going to die or what? This shit fucking hurts, dude."

Maybe.

"Demon!" I heard as the Huntress walked into the warehouse. I could hear the lightning still crackling between her fingers. "Come out, come out, wherever you are! You cannot escape your fate!"

I've been killed by every spell I know.

Your death won't be the end of you.

But there is a downside.

"Okay," I whispered as I hid behind a crate. I peered over it slowly, looking for the Huntress. "What's the downside?"

It's going to hurt more than anything in the forest.

"That isn't comforting."

It's better than dying your true death, boy.

"Show yourself, demon!" Her voice sent a chill up my spine. She was having fun. I could feel it in her words. "Or should I burn this place to the ground?"

"Why do they always become psychotic?" I whispered.

Because they want to kill you.

Stop speaking.

We don't know what other magic she's activated.

Good point.

Where the fuck is —

"There you are," said the Huntress as I looked up at her, following her boots up to her face. I brought flames to my arms to take the hit as she slammed her fists down on me, exploding the crate I was behind to bits as I rolled to the side. I quickly got to my feet and ran deeper into the warehouse. "Stay still, demon!" she called after me.

Go up. Hunters always go up.

They prefer to see all from a superior vantage point.

Get there before she does.

I nodded, jumping on some crates and pulling myself up onto an old walkway. I could hear the Huntress making her way to me. She wasn't far behind. I just prayed she didn't throw more lightning at me. The skylights weren't that far up. If I could just focus long enough on the flame inside me, I might be able to jump to the roof.

You won't get out of here without a fight.

Allow the flame to rage inside of you.

Ignoring Lordal, I let the heat grow within me before jumping again with a burst of fire. The move gave me the momentum

I needed and I crashed through one of the skylights. I landed ungracefully on the roof, nearly falling off before I saved myself. "Now what?" I said as I looked around.

Fight her.

"I don't want to fight her," I said, looking down at the abandoned lot next to the building. There were a few broken-down shipping trucks but other than that, there wasn't much else to see. From where I stood, they looked close enough for me to land on. I began hobbling towards them, calling upon the heat every step of the way to keep myself up right.

I don't understand why you're running.

Continuing to ignore Lordal, I leapt forward off the roof towards one of the trucks. I hit its side and bounced off, landing hard on my back against the ground. I groaned as I got to my feet, looking back at the building before I began to sneak away. "That wasn't so bad."

Idiot.

"Whatever," I said, just as the truck next to me exploded. I flew across the lot, my body torn apart by the explosion and debris that struck me. I was in too much pain to get back on my feet. I couldn't hear anything but the ringing in my ears, though Lordal's voice was clear in my mind.

My turn?

I was too weak to deny him. The lightning was still tearing at my side, and I clearly didn't stand a chance against the Huntress on my own. Even if I could have fought for control, I wouldn't have. I was too scared for my life to try.

"Your turn," I said, letting my consciousness enter our shared limbo, and the familiar heat began pumping through my veins once more.

LORDAL

I OPENED MY EYES TO SEE THE HUNTRESS WITH A bow in-hand, aiming a hell iron arrow at my chest. "You didn't think you'd get away that easily, did you?" she asked with a smile. She released the arrow, only for me to snag it out of the air before it hit me. I snapped the arrowhead off and stabbed it deep into her leg, forcing her to her knees. She screamed in pain, cursing at me as her leg began to bleed profusely. I got on my feet quickly, before she could surprise me with any more tricks. Her eyes burned with hatred. It seemed she understood now that I was not the boy. She looked up above us and I didn't take the bait, though I should have. She must have fired the arrow as soon as she'd exploded the truck, too quick for the boy to notice.

"You don't seem to understand," she said as the poison-coated arrow stabbed deep into my back, paralyzing me. She pushed herself up to her feet. "I'm helping you, demon. I'm ending your eternal suffering."

She reached into a pocket, revealing yet another spell box. Raising it to her lips, she whispered an incantation before slamming it down on her wound. She grimaced, pained by the process. The metal wrapped around her leg, forming a thick metal band to stop the bleeding. I looked her in the eyes as she unsheathed a sword I hadn't noticed under her robes. She rested the blade on my shoulder, as if I was being knighted. "At least die with honor, demon."

I nodded, respecting her request. The woman raised her sword then, bringing it down to my neck. Before it cut through, I allowed my body to be consumed by flames. I was a living inferno for just a second, long enough for her sword to cut through me without beheading me. Her blade was glowing red hot where it cut through the hellfire.

She dropped her robe behind her as she started forward, twirling the sword in her hand. My hands burst into flames as I readied myself for her next attack. The Huntress lunged forward, swinging the sword down on me. I stepped aside, pivoting around her and smashing a flaming trunk of a fist into the back of her head. Her body crumpled against the concrete before she groaned in pain and began to get back to her feet. I was surprised she wasn't already dead.

"Humans are such fragile creatures," I started, turning my back to her. "Yet you're all so high and mighty, as if I can't simply crush—"

Suddenly, pain shot through my spine as her holy blade ran through me from behind. I grunted, looking down at the blade of holy steel that had burst through my chest. The Huntress released the hilt and I turned to face her. She was stronger than I thought. I didn't expect her to get on her feet. She and I stood for a moment before accepting our injuries, both of us dropping to our knees from our respective wounds. We were both too weak to finish the other, though I found satisfaction in having delivered that fatal final strike.

"I'll kill you for this," I coughed, falling to my side. Blood dribbled down my cheek and covered my mouth. My eyes were fixed on the sky above us, the clouds drifting past as the steel burned its magic through my heart. "If I survive, you'll die."

For a moment, there was silence. I wondered if she'd expired after my last remark. Then, just as I assumed victory, the Huntress gasped before starting a furious coughing fit. When it finally passed, I heard her crunch the gravel beneath her feet as she stood back up.

"How?" I croaked as I stared in disbelief at her silhouette above me. I could feel the heat dying now, leaving my body as it grew colder and colder.

"Doesn't matter now, does it?" she said, before gripping the hilt of her sword. Before I could even attempt to do anything, she twisted the blade in my chest and shoved it deeper. "You're dead now, demon. What a fragile creature you are."

I felt the heat leave me. My eyes flickered shut as the world went black and the cold embrace of death claimed me once again.

* * * * * * *

IT WAS ONLY MOMENTS BEFORE I RETURNED FROM death. When I did, I saw the Huntress retrieving her robe from the rubble. Her sword was sheathed at her side.

I felt my chest as I rose up from the ground, looking at the spot where she had run me through. The wound was gone but the fresh bloodstains remained. The shirt I wore was torn to shreds from fighting the hellhounds, and it still smelled like shit from the sewers. Anthony Monroe was still my host. Which meant her ancestors must have killed me with the blade before. It was not capable of taking me from this life.

Just go, Lordal.

LORDAL

Get out of here before she notices.

Rage filled my mind. I couldn't turn down revenge. My path was hellfire and it burned through me entirely.

Lordal, please!

"Silence, boy," I demanded, walking towards the Huntress in an unsteady path. "Hey!"

The Huntress turned, reaching for her sword as her eyes widened in surprise. Before she could draw her weapon, I closed the distance between us, wrapping my right hand around her throat and lifting her. My left hand closed around hers on the hilt of her sword, crushing her bones with my grip. "You clearly don't know what I am," I said to her, watching the fear emerge in her eyes. I tossed her aside, unsheathing her sword as I separated her from it. She flew across the parking lot, crashing into the side of one of the trucks. She crumpled to the ground, blood dripping from a gash on her head. She was exhausted, I could tell from the way she was breathing. Clearly, her injuries were still affecting her, despite the show of bravado moments earlier.

She stayed down for a moment, long enough for me to walk over to her. Without a sound, the Huntress began to reach towards one of the many hidden compartments of her robe. Before she could retrieve whatever spell she intended to use, I raised my hands up. The heat flowed through me into the world. The flames from the earlier explosion leapt forward, landing directly onto her robe. It went up in flames, with her still wrapped inside. She began to scream as she rolled on the ground, trying to extinguish the flames that consumed her.

Lordal, stop!

Please don't do this!

I watched as the hellfire danced from her clothing to her skin, spreading across her flesh as it crackled with life. The life I had given it. The life I had taken from her. It consumed her very being. I was transforming her, making her the host of something greater than herself, no matter how fleeting its existence might be. I knew she would die but it meant the flame could live.

Lordal, please!

Please listen to me!

I tuned the boy's cries out, his words disrupting me as the woman screamed. She reached her hands towards me. I felt no sympathy as I watched her burn.

"Stop! Please! Please, stop!" the Huntress screamed as she managed to get up. She stumbled forward only a few steps before collapsing again. I wrapped my hand around her throat, her skin now blackened and cracked by the flames. I slammed her down into the remains of burning debris, leaving her there to die within the flames.

"Consider this your final lesson, hunter," I said, stabbing the holy blade into her gut. She let out one final cry of pain before her body went limp in my hand. Satisfied with my work, I dropped her there in the dirt.

ANTHONY

I SAT IN SILENCE ON THE SIDE OF THE ROAD, waiting for Joseph, attempting to make peace with Lordal's actions. He was a sociopathic monster just waiting to destroy the world. How could I live like this? I was foolish to think he could change his ways. This curse was heavy on my heart and mind. Maybe it would be easier if I just stayed away, let Lordal keep the vessel. I looked down at my bloody hands and thought back to Tyson in the locker room, his look of betrayal. To the woman in the Santa Monica alleyway, her body torn apart beyond recognition. I was finally starting to accept this power—understand this curse—but I simply couldn't understand the demon. I had to deal with the consequences of Lordal's choices. I needed to find a way, if there was a way, to make peace with that.

The crushing of gravel and the sound of a car horn came from up the alley, snapping me out of it. I looked up to see Joseph rolling up to me in his beaten down Jeep. He came to a stop in front of me, eyeing me up and down. Then he looked over to the burning remains of the warehouse Lordal and the Huntress destroyed in their battle. He pointed at the burning remains farther down the road and said, "So..."

"I don't want to talk about it," I mumbled as I opened the passenger door to get in, cutting him off. "Don't we have a hellhound to find?"

Joseph nodded, piecing together all that happened in his absence. It wasn't hard to figure out. Maybe he already knew and just feigned ignorance to appear human. The Oracle must have known what was going to happen, though maybe not. I didn't really care at the moment. I just wanted to leave it all behind.

"Okay, but before we go," said Joseph, reaching into the backseat. He placed a bundle of clothes and a beat-up pair of tactical boots down on the passenger seat in front of me. "Change. I'm not having you smell like blood, sweat, and shit the whole way there."

"Where exactly are we going?" I asked, beginning to change my shirt. I wiped the dirt from my face with the rag my old one had become.

The Jeep rumbled back to life as Joseph turned the engine over. He smiled knowingly over at me, a gesture only the host of the all-seeing Oracle could master. "You'll see."

SECTION 3

THE SLATS

ANTHONY

SWIRLING CLOUDS OF DUST KICKED UP BEHIND US as we raced across Mexico's deserts. I stared off at the barren landscape before us as the Jeep bumped over every crack in the earth. Not once did we discuss the burning mess we left behind. It wasn't something we needed to worry about anymore. There were clearly more important things to come.

"Do you even know where we're going?" I asked, looking over at Joseph. He'd been driving for almost a day now, refusing to let me take over. For whatever reason, he insisted he be the one to drive. I shrugged it off, assuming it had something to do with him being the Oracle. Maybe being "all-knowing" or whatever meant he never got tired. It definitely didn't look that way though. "Joseph," I said, still trying to get his attention.

He shook his head in response, before tapping the screen of the tracking device sitting between us. It refreshed, showing us two dots. One white and the other red. Joseph had explained earlier that we were the white one, and the red one was the hellhound with the tracker lodged in its skin.

"You ask a lot of questions. I'm just following the map." Joseph stayed fixated on the road, his eyes glazed over. He nodded, confirming what he said to be true for no apparent reason before repeating himself again. "I'm just following the map."

I assumed it was Oracle-related spacing out and didn't think too much of it. My mind was focused on other things, like where we were going, or more importantly, what would happen when we got there. For all I knew, we were driving into a trap. Or worse, a pack of hellhounds. It had taken all we had to fight just one. I had to assume Joseph knew we weren't driving to our death.

I also found myself wanting answers about everything: about why the Oracle had shown me that book, about the Hands of the Apocalypse, about why I'd seen those visions, but Joseph swore he didn't know what I was shown, and the Oracle wasn't giving him answers. Something about the process kept even Lordal away from the knowledge. He had no idea that I knew him now, who he was and what he could become. I thought it was better if I didn't tell him. When he asked what I'd seen, I lied and said the details were fuzzy. It seemed even he was aware that the Oracle's visions were protected from his perception.

Lordal and I did properly discuss our run-ins with hunters though. He let me know back-to-back encounters hadn't happened to him in over a century. His best guess was that something had emerged to bring them together, and he feared we would soon figure out what it was. With hellhounds running around so freely, he worried the war the Oracle warned us about could soon drag us into it. I had to remind him that we were already part of it. I was stuck in a Jeep driving across Mexico when I would have rather been anywhere else.

Lordal grumbled before falling silent again. I looked ahead of us out the window, watching the landscape outside continue to blend together as we sped by. I found my mind wandering through everything I'd experienced since the demon had arrived. Pain, suffering, loss. The rage. Nothing good, it seemed. My life had evolved in such a way that I could no longer recognize it. I stared ahead, thinking about the possibilities of what was about to unfold when we finally arrived at our destination.

My daydreams were interrupted by the tracker screen suddenly beeping. I looked up at Joseph, whose attention snapped down immediately. He pointed at the red dot on the screen as the Jeep slowed. "There we go," he mumbled mostly to himself, slamming his foot on the gas.

* * * * * * *

HALF AN HOUR LATER, THE JEEP ROLLED TO A stop, crunching gravel as it came to rest just before the edge of a cliff. Below us was a massive valley. "It's here," said Joseph, turning off the engine and his tracker.

"Okay, but…" The sun was beginning to rise, illuminating the valley below. I could only vaguely see structures and rock formations below us. We hopped out of the Jeep, our boots kicking up the rocks beneath us. "Where are we?"

Joseph came up beside me and took in a deep breath in awe. "I have no idea," he said, exhaling. Below us, spreading across the valley of rock and sand, were the ruins of an ancient civilization, destroyed long ago by the desert storms. Broken statues were revealed as the sun continued to rise higher into the sky. I could just make out wings on the backs of some, but it was impossible to tell from this distance if they were upon the backs of angels or demons.

"It's beautiful," I admitted as the sunlight revealed it all.

"The hellhound's down there somewhere," said Joseph, gesturing towards the valley before us. He turned and made his way to the back of the Jeep, leaving me at the edge of the valley.

"Do you know what this place is?" I asked Lordal.

The Slats.

A dark place, one filled with nightmares.

We should not be here.

He sank back into silence as if he'd never spoken, his words living on in my mind. I couldn't help but feel something was wrong with this whole situation. I suddenly felt like a pawn in a game of chess being moved into position by an unseen hand. We were just following invisible guides, blind to the rest of the board.

The one thing still bothering me was why the hellhound left the city when it did. It seemed too convenient, considering one had worn out Lordal. If the second had attacked after the fight with the Huntress, it would have won. Instead, it ran. The question plagued my mind and Lordal offered no resolution. I couldn't help but feel as though something much bigger was going on, and whatever it was, I was certain it would reveal itself to us down in that valley.

The Slats. The words echoed in my thoughts as the sun rose over the horizon. It was nearly fully in view. I raised a hand to shield my eyes against the early morning light.

I knew this place once.

Long before it became what you see now.

Before it was this wasteland.

Do you know what happened?

These people sealed their fate.

They made it into what it is.

And what did it become? I asked as Joseph returned from the Jeep with a pair of binoculars in his hand. He perched up on the ledge, looking down into the valley.

A place of ancient satanic worship.

They allowed it to become a gateway to Hell.

I looked out into the valley over Joseph's shoulder. The grim reality of this place was setting in quickly. If Lordal was right, somewhere out there was a way into Hell itself.

"Jesus, this place is a mess," muttered Joseph, still using the binoculars. He leaned forward as he looked deeper in the ruins, pointing with his free hand. He handed the binoculars up to me. "There's the hellhound," he said, pointing into the valley.

I took the binoculars from his hand and peered through, focusing where he pointed. A dust cloud trailed behind the beast, obscuring it from view. I could just make out the same blood-red fur I'd seen back in Mexico City.

"Yup, there's our hellhound," I said, looking ahead to see where it was heading. "Where's it going?"

I saw a ruined temple. It was clear that this was the hellhound's intended destination. What remained of the temple was mostly unimpressive rubble, though it had clearly fared better than every other structure down there. The valley itself looked like it had all been through Hell, and with the knowledge I now had, I was sure it had been. Everything except this one structure was destroyed completely, and the hellhound was making its way straight towards it.

"There's something else down there," I told Joseph, spotting something just in front of the temple. I watched as the hellhound slowed to a stop near the entrance of the structure. There was a dark statue standing before the entryway, blocking the beast's path.

The hound cowered away from the figure, seemingly distraught by the encounter. It lurched its head back and howled. In response, the statue came to life, suddenly raising its hand up to the creature, and the hellhound fell silent. The hand of the statue waved it forward, clearly permitting the beast to enter. Then I realized it wasn't a statue at all. The way its body flowed and shifted so smoothly when it had silenced the hellhound. I couldn't place it but I had seen it somewhere before.

The hellhound approached cautiously, cowering away from the figure before it scrambled past it towards the entrance. Once it had cleared the figure, the hellhound darted inside, disappearing from view. I cursed under my breath, realizing we were most likely going in after it. The figure outside the temple returned to its original position, its hands clasped together before its waist.

The morning light continued to slowly rise over the ruins. I stayed fixated on the figure at the entrance as the light washed over it. Layers of darkness began to evaporate into mist around it, vanishing into the air to reveal the form of a man underneath. The shadows that remained began to wrap around him, forming a cloak and hood. Once his transformation was complete, the man turned and looked up directly at me. It caused me to stumble backwards into Joseph.

"What the hell?" said Joseph, pushing me away from him as I fell back. "What? What happened?"

"What the fuck was that?" I shouted, catching my balance. I looked back down at the man in front of the temple. His eyes met mine again and his mouth began to move. He was saying something.

Shadows crept forward from the entry of the temple, floating past him in a rolling fog. It didn't seem that he was surrounded by them; rather, it was as if he was the shadows. There was no distinction of where they ended and his form began. It was as though they were moving around him not because he wanted them too, but because they were drawn to him.

The man below tilted his head, as if he was confused by me. He spoke again, and this time I knew what he said.

"He's saying my name." I turned to Joseph, getting up and handing him the binoculars. "He's saying my fucking name."

"That doesn't make any sense," said Joseph, shaking his head in confusion. He brought the binoculars up to his eyes, looking down into the valley for what I'd seen.

I was already gone. I started off down a path into the valley, figuring out a route to the temple. I threw my hands up in the air. My blood was boiling. "Everywhere I go," I shouted on my way down. "Everywhere I fucking go, man."

* * * * * * *

JOSEPH RETURNED TO THE JEEP BEFORE HE JOINED me. He had his backpack full of gear with him, and his shotgun slung over his shoulder. "Anthony!" he called after me. "Slow down!"

I turned around and waited for him to catch up. He stumbled as he reached me, winded from his jog. He rested his hand on my shoulder, taking a moment to breathe. "You can't just rush into shit anymore," he said between breaths. "You exist in a different world now, man. Someone's always going to be trying to trick you into a deal or trying to kill you. You need to think before you act, otherwise you're no different from Lordal. And look what happened to him. Cursed." He patted my shoulder as his breathing returned to normal. "It's great that you're learning to use your power but don't let it blind you. You don't know what can happen, or what you'll come up against. The deeper you get into the supernatural, the more dangerous things are going to become."

Joseph paused but we both knew what he meant. I understood what he meant. With the gift of Lordal's power also came his rage. His rage burned a begging woman to death. It didn't matter that she was trying to kill us. There had to have been a better way to handle her, but I had lost control. I couldn't retake the body. It didn't matter how many lives we saved if Lordal killed everyone that got in his way. If I couldn't fight that rage—that need for violence—nothing we ever did would matter.

My mind was burdened with more than just the Huntress's death. Lordal had killed the hellhound in the sewers. Before that, we'd killed the Hunter in the woods. I thought back to Santa Monica, to those people. Deep down, I knew their faces. I'd seen what Lordal did to them, and I would never tell another living soul. And he knew that I'd seen it, that I'd bore witness to his chaos. To his evil. To his sin. Tyson was dead because of it. I owed it to him, to all of Lordal's victims, to control the demon.

"You're right," I said, looking back at Joseph. "You're right."

I paused, noticing then just how fast I was moving, how far I'd made it into the ruins. I needed to stop and think, to gather myself and form a plan. No wonder Joseph needed to catch his breath. I looked at him, panting and trudging along with his gear over his back. He isn't like me, I reminded myself. We were both hosts but mine healed me, gave me strength. Mine made me nearly immortal. His would let him die and simply move on to the next host. If Joseph died because of my mistakes, I would never be able to forgive myself. He had helped me. He was my only friend in this strange new life I was living.

Just because I could do all of these amazing things now didn't mean everyone else could. It was something I needed to understand.

I took Joseph's backpack from him, throwing it over one shoulder and putting his arm over the other, helping him walk the rest of the way to the temple. Even now, I could feel myself using my power. The tiniest flame growing inside me. I really hadn't stopped to think about just how powerful I had become, or what that power now meant.

"You have no idea what we're walking into," said Joseph as we approached the temple. Ahead of us, the figure stood just inside the shadow of the ruins, cast down from above and reaching the clearing's edges.

"You're the one that brought us here," I reminded him as I stopped us at the edge of where the sunlight ended and the shadow of the temple began.

"Anthony Monroe," the man called out. He raised his hand toward us, inviting us to come closer. I didn't trust the shadows around him. "Come forward. We are not strangers, for we have met before."

"Sorry, man. I think you've got the wrong guy." I looked up at the man, having been distracted by the temple's shadow. It seemed to move, almost like a spilled fluid across the ground. It was spreading slowly, then suddenly reformed into its original form as we neared. "I think I'd remember meeting someone like you."

The man lowered his hood, revealing his face along with his dark hair and clean-shaven face. He was young—younger than I imagined. He looked to be in his thirties but I could no longer guess someone's age. For all I knew, he was thousands of years old. His tanned skin spoke to his obvious time spent in the desert. "Hello, Oracle," said the man with a nod of his head, ignoring me. "It's good to see you again."

"I don't know you either," said Joseph. "I only know what you are. But the memories I have of you... Those memories aren't mine. You may as well give us a proper introduction."

"My name is Luka," he said, gesturing to himself with both hands. "I am the vessel of the Shadow, and I have served as its host since its arrival here on Earth."

"We have met before," I mumbled, remembering the phantom figure that abducted me from the redwood forest. "In the woods, after the Hunter. You brought me to Mexico. Why? And what the hell are you doing here?"

"You already know why." Luka paused, interrupted by an eerie howl from deep within the temple. The sound vibrated through the structure, amplified as it escaped out into the ruins. Silence fell over us and the hairs on my neck and arms were left standing as the noise echoed away.

"The war." Luka broke the silence. "A prelude to the end brought me to this place. The darkness... I can feel it shifting. There is growing unrest in Hell. It drew me to the gates. It seems fitting that we all find ourselves here. The balance shifts, even now."

"What do you mean?" I asked, annoyed that every entity I'd met was so cryptic. I looked back at Joseph, who had crouched to the ground. I had to make sure I wasn't missing something. He just shrugged. I wasn't all that comforted by the fact that we were both lost.

"We must destroy the Devil," said Luka. "His power grows to its peak. His wrath will soon be felt by mankind if we do not intervene."

"What're you talking about? What does the Devil have to do with this?" Joseph asked, standing up beside me. He was suddenly looking livelier. "What does Lucifer have to do with any of this?"

I realized then just how clueless he was to the visions the Oracle showed me. If he knew what I'd seen, he'd know the role Lucifer played in the creation of Lordal. Perhaps this was how it began. The beginning of the end. This place, these two entities, could all be connected to the vision I had of the world in flames. What we did here now could very well decide the fate of the Earth.

"It started here. This is where the Lord sent him." Luka gestured to the ruins around us. "This is where Lucifer fell."

I stepped forward, into the swimming pool of shadows. "Tell us," I demanded. "Tell us everything."

****

WHEN LUCIFER WAS BANISHED FROM THE Heavens, there was no Hell. Only the Earth existed, where the

Lord made man, and so He sent Lucifer here to learn from man's innocence. But Lucifer, in his hatred for his Father's creations, chose a darker path.

Long before it was known as the Slats, the place had a different name. Then, it was known as the Garden. It was here that Lucifer came, and it was here that became the birthplace of all temptation, of mankind's original sin. There was no more faith for those who entered the Garden. It became the Devil's land, and it was no place for men to venture. Still, brave fools came to face the angel that had fallen.

The Devil spent centuries in the Garden, harvesting the souls of those he slaughtered like perennial flowers, building his power, savoring it. Until he decided he needed his own kingdom to challenge the Heavens, and the Creator.

Lucifer—with a new power that rivaled that of the Lord himself—tore through the very fabric of existence, of reality, and became a Creator himself. He created his kingdom, where he could rule and grow his powers. The Heavens were filled with light, so Lucifer chose to fill Hell with darkness.

However, in his vendetta against the Lord, Lucifer felt compelled to return to Earth. He brought forth the hellfire from his new kingdom, with which he tainted his Father's creations, creating demons from the burning flesh of mankind. Demons that served him, as angels served the Lord. His spawn plagued the Earth, collecting souls forevermore to build the fallen angel's power.

* * * * * * *

I WAITED FOR MORE, THOUGH IT SEEMED LUKA was done with his story. I shook my head at the entirety of the tale. "What the fuck does that have to do with anything? Or any of us?" I nearly yelled at him.

"Don't forget your place, Anthony Monroe. You are only a host. You are disposable." He was the first one to say it to my face, though I had understood that fact since the first time I died in the redwood forest. It wasn't me that mattered in this nightmare. It was always Lordal. My stomach turned as Luka nodded his head in approval of my silence. "Now," he continued, "it's time we have him join us."

Luka opened his arms, as if preparing to embrace me. I thought I was going to be flung into his arms but I stayed where I stood. The heat inside me began to swell, flashing my body with a sudden and viscous sweat. I groaned as my temperature continued to rise, the heat causing me to drop lower to the ground as I grew disoriented. I was brought to my knees as my vision blurred, as the world started to spin around me. My own flesh quickly grew unbearable to be in, my skin beginning to glow. I screamed out in pain as my body suddenly burst into flames.

"What are you doing to me?" I screamed at Luka as the flames continued to envelop me. "Help me, Joseph! Make it stop!"

I heard Joseph shout, then Luka speak, but I couldn't understand. Whatever was said between them was enough for Joseph to watch me burn. Then the flames began to trail off of me, the heat leaving my flesh. It took shape before me, wrapping and knitting together into a being of pure fire. The being screamed in agony from within the fire, collapsing to its knees. The flames began to take the form of flesh.

The fire completely left me then and I collapsed into the dirt, exhausted by the ordeal. I felt so cold now that I understood what was happening. I laid there staring in awe as the man continued to form, his face finally emerging from the flames. I knew who he was, although I had never truly seen his face before. We had been speaking for a long time though.

Lordal bellowed as the flames were completely absorbed into his form. He collapsed next to me, naked except for the shackles on his wrists. His scarred body was completely revealed to us all. He forced himself up with a mighty groan, getting on his feet. He looked at his own body as he stood, clearly baffled by having his body again.

Joseph walked over to me slowly, his eyes glued to Lordal. He helped me stand and we all stood in silence, until Lordal and I turned to Luka and asked the same question in unison: "What the hell did you do?"

LORDAL

I CALLED UPON THE FLAMES TO CREATE MY customary black and red armor while we waited for answers. "Speak, Shadow," I demanded as the flames dissipated. "I need answers."

"I answer only to a higher power," said the Shadow. He was seated at the entryway of the temple, suddenly deeply focused on his meditation. I wondered for a moment what could be so powerful that it allowed him the power to bend the curse's hold over my soul. Certainly not the God that let this happen to me in the first place.

"There's nothing stopping me now from turning you to ash," I reminded him.

"You can try," said the Shadow without even opening his eyes. "The hellfire that carries your essence has taken the form of your body. Using your power will only weaken you."

The Shadow seemed to be speaking the truth. Creating my armor did make me feel strange. I assumed it was because I was unaccustomed to my own flesh, but perhaps this form was unstable. "Then what are we doing here?" I asked. "Why bring me to the gates of Hell? If it's true what you say, if I am too weak to face you, fighting Lucifer will simply be the death of me."

The boy was quiet. He seemed to be piecing something together, though I didn't know what. He was a fool without my guidance. I remembered then that the Oracle had shown him visions. I knew he was lying to me about not being able to remember, but if this was familiar to him… "Oracle," I said calmly, facing St. Claire. "How long have you known?" St. Claire's eyes widened as I continued. "Or have you been leading us on the entire time?"

I needed to be careful with my rage. It would only serve to weaken me. I was suddenly aware of the weight of the shackles on my wrists—aware that the Shadow had put them on me himself. I wasn't free at all. We were still just pawns in their game.

"What're you talking about, Lordal?" the boy asked. He rose up off a fallen pillar he was leaning against. "Why are we here?"

"This is where I died my first death." I exhaled some of my rage, fighting my desire to strangle St. Claire. "Where I was born again in Lucifer's image."

"The birthplace of the first demon," said the Shadow.

"I should kill you for lying to me," I roared at St. Claire. He tripped over some rubble as I lunged at him.

"I— I—" he stuttered, falling to the ground. "I—"

"I don't want to hear it!"

"Lordal!" said the boy as he came between us. "Calm down! We would be dead without Joseph!"

"You truly are a fool," I said to the boy as I shoved him aside. "They needed you to bring me here. You've done your job. They don't need you anymore."

I finally understood. Joseph St. Claire kept the boy alive to save themselves from the trouble of finding me again. The

Shadow sent us straight to the Oracle. We've only ever been pawns in their fucking game.

"They've been lying to us," I said, pointing down at the Oracle's host. "We made a detour in Mexico so that St. Claire could have his revenge on his little hellhound. We probably didn't need to track the second hellhound at all, did we?" Joseph shook his head, muttering to himself under his breath as he cowered. "Get up, you split-brained shit," I said as I picked him up by his collar. "I should just walk away. Leave you two to your mess."

"You can't," said the Shadow. I turned to see him standing at the entryway, his arms crossed over his chest. He stared into my would-be soul as he said, "You must descend before it's too late—before we're all doomed."

I saw the truth in his hazel eyes. He was simply reminding me of what I already knew—of everything at stake, not just mankind. Mankind could go extinct for all I cared, but the Shadow knew that. It had been a few lifetimes since we last met. We had agreed to be allies then, though now I wasn't sure I could trust him. I wasn't sure I could trust anyone. I let go of my hold on St. Claire, slightly weakened by my rage.

"We will be at your side in the end," said the Shadow, as if he was in my head. "But you must find out the Devil's plans. We can only help you from the shadows until then."

I nodded, looking back at St. Claire and the boy.

"What's wrong?" the boy asked.

"Nothing," I lied. I knew deep down everything was falling apart. My plan was falling apart entirely and coming together at the same time, and I had no idea what to expect moving forward. I never expected to cooperate in some grand scheme for the Devil's demise. I had always planned—still planned—on killing him myself. I turned back to the Shadow as I said, "Fine. I will have you all by my side in the end."

"Thank you, Lordal," said the Shadow.

"Thanks," said St. Claire quietly, rubbing his collarbone in an uncomfortable fashion.

"I only ask that when he comes for us," I started, looking at all three of them one at a time. "I'm the one that ends him. I want to tear his heart out. I want to watch whatever light there might be in him leave his eyes."

They all nodded slowly. The boy understood my hatred, how deep it ran, as he had felt it himself many times. Now, perhaps, he was beginning to understand where it came from. The other two simply knew what it meant to me. "Then lead the way," I said to the Shadow as we entered the temple. "Take us to the gateway."

ANTHONY

WE PASSED THE REMAINS OF A STATUE, THEN crushed and crumbling stone pews. It felt like time flowed through here at all points: the beginning and the end of the temple. I could hear echoes of laughter in the halls, then screams and cries for help. Shadows skittered across the walls, leaping across the cracked dome ceiling high above us. I doubted that they belonged to Luka. I wondered if it was what remained of the worshippers, somehow. The walls were covered in unfamiliar symbols and depictions of the Devil, with massive runes carved where stained glass windows would have usually been.

I knew the place felt familiar when we were outside. I had seen it before mankind built their structures here. It was once the forest where Orm Gon became Lordal.

The temple smelled like shit, much worse than Joseph or I did from our time in the sewers. It comforted me a little but I was still panicking. Surely it was hellhound shit, but what if it was something worse? Without Lordal, I was just a twenty-two-year-old college dropout. I wasn't meant to be here with these powerful entities, participating in a plot against the Devil. I was surprised no one told me to stay behind. I couldn't see the future or control shadows, and I wasn't a demon. I wasn't even Lordal's host right now. I was clearly dead weight but if they didn't ask me to stay behind, there must have been a reason. Unless they just really didn't care. They had already made it clear that I was disposable.

Joseph had told me the Oracle couldn't see my future and even if he had betrayed our trust, I believed him. Maybe not the Oracle, but Joseph St. Claire. The visions I received had shown me Lordal's future clear as day. He was free and I wasn't with him. That didn't seem to leave many options for what could have happened to me.

We reached a set of big iron doors, damaged by massive claw marks and numerous scorches. Lordal stepped forward to try and pry them open but Luka stopped him. He raised his hand toward the doors, pushing them forward with a flick of his wrist. They flew open, slamming into the walls. Rocks toppled from the impact somewhere in the Slats. "Save your strength," he told Lordal.

The doors led us to a spiral staircase stretching so far down that the steps were swallowed by darkness. There was no way to tell how deep it went. Lordal held a flame in his hand, illuminating the way. We began our descent, one step at a time, with Lordal one step ahead. The flame that burned from his hand crackled and snapped as we moved in silence. I looked at the dimly lit walls around us. They were covered in carvings and what appeared to be scripture, though it wasn't a language I had ever seen before. The carvings varied. Some were more primitive than others. The deeper we got, the more diverse the carvings and scripture became. The only thing that remained the same were the deep scratches that became more and more plentiful as we continued to descend deeper and deeper into the Earth.

We passed a depiction of a black circle forming some sort of altar, to which the simple stick figures were bowing. Another showed a bunch of demons with small heads and massive bodies chasing stick figures from below, back up the way we came. The fact that it was clear it was demons chasing people rattled me. I shivered as chills washed over me.

"Are we sure this is safe?" I had to ask. "Us being down here?"

"No," the entities said in unison, causing me to pause. They continued on and I quickly snapped myself out of it, before the darkness surrounded me.

For a moment, I wondered if we were actually walking to the Gates of Hell. Joseph and Luka had fooled us once. They could still be plotting against us now. Surely, Lordal thought so too. I hoped so, at least.

The flame in Lordal's hand extinguished. "What the hell?" I heard him say up ahead. Suddenly, he let out a deep cry as his voice faded into the darkness. Something shifted ahead of us. I heard a whisper. Then I felt a breeze, as if we weren't deep underground. The singular whisper became more, a harmony of whispers, and they were coming closer with every panicked breath I took. There was a horrifying shriek from a chamber in front of us. Joseph flicked on a small flashlight and we made our way forward. We needed to find Lordal.

A low growl greeted us as we entered the chamber. "Should we kill them?" a voice croaked from the darkness. Skittering noises, like rats in walls, started above our heads.

"What do we do?" I whispered to Joseph. His response was to grab my hand in the dark. I heard him unsheathe his knife from his belt. It was the only reason I was certain that it was what he placed into my hand. I didn't need to see it to know. "Okay," I whispered nervously.

I was immediately reminded that I should not be here, with or without a knife. I was going to be the first one dead if I didn't run back up those stairs. Before I could decide to fight or run, something flew over us, smashing into the wall above the entryway. It collapsed to the ground and we turned. Joseph shined his flashlight down at the mass on the floor in front of us. Lordal's arm had been ripped off, the blood pooling beneath his remains. Both of his legs had been broken so badly that I could see bones. They were bent unnaturally. His neck was broken. His organs were slowly spilling out of him from deep, massive slashes. I stared in shock at the mighty demon's corpse. I could hear the shallow breathing of the monsters as they grew closer. No doubt they believed the real threat was taken care of, and they weren't wrong. We were nothing compared to the fury of Lordal. I was nothing at all—just a guy with a knife trying not to piss himself in the dark. At least I wasn't the first one dead. That was something.

"Anthony!" said Joseph as he smacked my head. "Pay attention. Breathe. Come on, man."

Luka was already retreating, looking around wildly at what we couldn't see. Joseph let me go ahead of him. Before I even reached Lordal's remains, a long gray clawed hand reached down, snatching at my neck and hoisting me up. I screamed as I was pulled upwards, dropping my knife immediately. I could feel the heavy breathing on my face as the monster brought its face to mine. Its teeth clattered together as it opened its mouth, forcing me to smell its disgusting breath. With the light cast from Joseph's flashlight, I could slightly make out its grotesque form.

"Release the boy!" shouted Luka, and a blinding light filled the room. The creature hissed in my face, dropping me while I was still blinded. I stumbled forward as the room grew dark again. Someone came up beside me. Joseph told me to relax, to walk with him. I could hear something scurrying frantically behind us. I wobbled as I rubbed my eyes, unable to believe the sight of the disgusting monster chasing us.

Joseph let off two shots with his shotgun, blasting the creature back when it suddenly sprang forward. The flash from the gunshots illuminated enough of the room beyond the monster to show us how fucked we really were. The whole chamber was full of them. They all had gray, wet-looking skin. Like the first one, the others crawled forward, from above and below and across the walls. Rags covered their bodies, makeshift cloaks made of ancient fabrics. They had no eyes though they still made their way toward us with ease.

Joseph's first shot had sent them all into a frenzy. Their cries were like nothing I had ever heard before, so unnatural I didn't know if I could ever describe it. Joseph's second shot had just pissed them off. They all roared in unison as they rushed us. I turned, sprinting up the stairs back to the surface.

We were done here. This was over. We lost.

LORDAL

I GROANED AS I CAME BACK TO LIFE, CONFUSED BY the silence. Wraiths were ugly, annoying creatures. They were loud. If it was quiet, I was alone. The fools ran off without me, leaving me for dead.

The flames restored me, burned through my veins. My blood like gasoline hit with a spark. My bones fused back together. I stared into the darkness, reminded of the abyss. I almost wished I was still dead. It would allow me to rest, if only for a little longer. "Do they know?" I asked.

"No. Hopefully they never will." The Shadow stepped out of the dark, raising a glowing ball of pure white light in his hand. He kneeled beside me, bringing the light down to inspect my injuries. He watched as my crippled form stitched itself back together. "The new Oracle is still learning, and he can't see the past. How long until you're ready?"

I turned away from him, looking at the center of the chamber. There stood a slab of pure hellstone: the Gateway to Hell. Its presence in this desert valley was the very reason the Slats had been built here. It had spawned here the same day I was transformed into the being I was now. Its power echoed through me, welcoming me.

"What if I'm too weak?" I asked, sitting up as my upper body finished healing. "What if all this planning only ends in failure?"

"You'll die," he said plainly, rising to his feet. "Then you'll return, and we'll try again until it's too late to try anymore. You're still cursed, Lordal."

The Shadow made his way toward the slab. When he reached it, he released his light, allowing it to float next to him so he could rest his hands on the ancient stone. I flinched as he touched it. If he wasn't such a powerful entity, it would have burned him on contact.

"You still don't understand," he said over his shoulder. His hands danced over the stone. "Do you know why you — of all entities — were chosen?"

"No," I admitted. I grunted then as my legs began to regain feeling and my spine fused back together. I shoved myself off the ground as I recreated my armor. I joined the Shadow at the slab. I leaned against it; my strength drained from healing myself. Then I sank to the ground beside him, leaning my back against the hellstone. We didn't speak for a moment. I still didn't know if I could do this. Eight thousand years of hatred boiled inside me. Centuries of pain, suffering, and loss. I sank deeper and deeper into my hatred for the Devil, my rage boiling just beneath the surface.

The Shadow stared into the slab, seemingly lost in its deep darkness. He suddenly shifted beside me and I saw him climb up on the stone, inspecting it below his feet. I was convinced that now he would surely die from touching the gateway. Still, nothing happened to him, and he turned to me with his hands behind his back. "Only one soul remained in the Garden when Hell was created — Lucifer's Champion," he started. "You, the first demon."

"I know. I was there."

"You aren't funny."

"Speak plainly, Shadow. Enough of your games."

The Shadow's orb of light returned to his hand as he banished the darkness away. "You're dumber than I'd like. I didn't choose you, fool. Hell did."

"What do you mean?" I asked, my blood boiling slightly at the Shadow calling me a fool.

"When Hell was created, it wasn't made as a part of the known universe." The Shadow hopped off the slab. "It rests between this one and the next, connecting worlds. And much like our own, it needed a champion—a guardian to protect it."

"Are you telling me that I'm a cosmic entity?"

"You are nothing like me," said the Shadow as he walked out of the chamber. "You are, however, blessed with great power. Comparable, perhaps, to my own."

"Then why am I bound to an idiot boy? Why do I only exist as a parasite? Why am I weakened by the likes of you?"

"Because you're cursed, Lordal. The Devil holds the key to your true gifts. He is the barrier between you and the power within."

"I don't understand."

"Hell is your birthright. It chose you to rule it, not the false king that sits on the throne now. Lucifer is nothing more than an outsider to the realm that created you. He is from the Heavens, and thus had no business creating Hell. His new realm needed an anchor, and so it was you that was chosen. He sought to control you, to control the only power that might stand a chance at destroying him, because you are Lordal, the Champion of Hell."

Luka vanished and his light faded away with him, leaving me alone with my thoughts. Flames rose from my hands to illuminate the chamber around me. Frustration and anger boiled inside of me, driving me mad. The heat flared and I felt my heart begin to ache as the fire grew within. I climbed on top of the hellstone slab and it immediately began to burn, a black ring of fire forming along the edge. I stood in the middle, only thinking of one thing: killing Lucifer.

The flames began to close, leaping forward, drawn to me by my demonic life force. They consumed me like no fire ever had, burning me down to my atoms. The process was the most painful I had ever experienced, yet I made no effort to scream. My body crumbled to ashes as the flames finished their task, and my soul sank to the depths of Hell.

ANTHONY

THE CREATURES SHRIEKED BEHIND US AS WE RAN up the stairs. We reached the surface and ran past the iron doorway that Luka had forced open earlier. Joseph pulled a small green box from his pocket, yanking on its string before tossing it into the stairwell behind us. When it exploded, I slowed down thinking we were safe, but the shrieking continued. "What the hell are those things?" I asked as I followed Joseph.

"Wraiths," he said as he placed another small box at a doorway. The creatures emerged from the darkness then and rushed us, crashing into an invisible barrier as the small box bounced from their impact. They instantly began to pound against it, trying to tear their way into the chamber we were in. "That's only going to give us a minute or two," he said as he caught his breath. "We need to keep moving."

I was still catching my breath as the small box rattled from the slamming of the monsters' bodies. I could see them clearly now. They had no eyes or ears, only their mouths to scream. "They look like zombies."

"No, not zombies." Joseph sucked on his teeth as he tried to explain. "They're more, like, tortured souls given physical form, and their physical form is—" The wraiths slammed against the barrier with such force that the small box cracked in half. "Well, that."

"You have more of those, right?"

"No. Keep running."

The barrier broke before we made it out of the temple. Joseph pushed me to take cover behind a stone pew as the horde rushed inside. The wraiths clawed up to the ceiling, up walls and columns. One fell from above and landed in front of me, its hood falling back to reveal its disturbing face. Their screams echoed all around us as I kicked out, knocking the creature away. I scrambled backwards as the thing tackled me to the ground, raising its claws to slash me to pieces. I cried out one last time as its guts exploded all over me, chunks of it falling into my mouth. The wraith fell on top of me and I gagged as I spit out its blood. Joseph hoisted me up, pulling me out from under the monster, and I vomited.

"Now is not the time, Anthony," said Joseph as he fired another shell.

I looked up at him as I wiped my mouth clean. The monsters were swarming us. "I don't have Lordal's power!" I reminded him over the wraiths' screams. "What are we going to do?"

"I'm looking for a door to the Manor!" said Joseph as he reloaded his shotgun. "Do you see one?"

I did a quick scan of the room, hoping to see the beautiful door I'd seen in Mexico City. There was nothing.

Joseph fired at an incoming wraith, blasting it to bits in midair. The creatures rushed us again, grabbing Joseph and yanking him over the pews as more descended. Some lunged for me then. The only thing I could do was close my eyes and pray that it was a painless death.

There was no sound. Everything was dark. I must have died my last death — my true death. It happened so fast I didn't even feel it. Then I opened my eyes.

Luka stood at the entryway of the temple, where we met him. He had his hands raised, holding them out toward the creatures. The wraiths cowered, silently retreating to the stairwell they chased us out of. Luka waited for them all to be out of sight, then he lowered his hands and walked out into the valley. "Oh," said Joseph, mostly to himself. Then, loud enough for me to hear, he said, "They fear him."

Before I could say anything, the wraiths began their charge again. They must have known Luka walked out and wasted no time resuming their pursuit. "Let's get the fuck out of here," said Joseph, pushing me forward.

We ran out as the creatures exploded back into the temple with ferocity, desperate to tear us to shreds.

LORDAL

MY SOUL FOUND MY BODY AS IT REFORMED. I collapsed to the ground, catching myself with an extended arm. Smoke rolled off my body as I rose, taking in the view. Despite being its Champion, I'd never actually set foot in the fiery kingdom. I was doomed to Earth, from host to host.

Thick dense wisps of smog drifted around the slab of hellstone I'd spawned upon. I stepped off as a familiar howl echoed through the fog. It was the sound of a hellhound, though now there was no way for me to know if it was the same one from the sewers. I didn't have St. Claire's tracker and there were countless hounds here. I struggled to look through the fog as shadows shifted around me.

"Why have you come, Lordal?" The Devil's voice roared in my head and all around me. It roared in Hell entirely.

"Powerful beings seek your destruction, Lucifer," I shouted as I stepped away from the gateway. The smog was so thick that breathing was harsh on my lungs. Being on Earth weakened me to Hell's environment. "They've sent me to make an attempt on your life—to strike you down and claim the throne."

I made my way through the haze, nothing visible beyond my own hands. I called upon the flame, sparking to life a small fire in the palm of my hand. Holding it up, I tried to see farther ahead, but it was no use. The fog covered everything, shrouding the world around me. I wondered if it was Lucifer keeping my eyes off of my birthright.

I smelled a familiar stench and ducked as a hellhound soared over me. It vanished back into the unknown. The beast smelled of shit, exactly like the boy and St. Claire. It was the same hound, trying to hide in the dense fog around me.

"Face me yourself, Lucifer!" I shouted. There was no reason to fear the beast. I could smell exactly where it was, even if I couldn't see it with my own eyes.

Lucifer chuckled as the hellhound revealed itself. It tilted its head to the side as it spoke in his voice. "Can't you see it, Lordal?" it asked. "I've always been here."

The beast lunged forward, its jaws snapping in the air as I stepped aside. I reached out, snapping the hound's neck before it thudded to the ground, its eyes lifeless. Its corpse vanished from my sight as the fog creeped over it.

"Enough of your games!" I shouted out to the tyrant that ruled over Hell. "Enough of this nonsense! Face me now, Devil!"

The ground rumbled. Suddenly, the earth gave way beneath me and I fell through the ceiling of a throne room. Massive statues of Lucifer himself decorated the walkway. Gold and obsidian lined the walls, forming columns and molding. As I pushed myself from the floor, the ceiling pieced itself together, as if I'd never fallen through. I looked up only to find that the ceiling was already repaired.

"Welcome home," I heard from behind me. I turned to face Lucifer as he rose from his throne. "Lordal."

I brushed myself off as the crater I created from my landing repaired itself. Lucifer's defenses were impressive.

"Why are you here, demon?" the Devil continued, stepping forward as he questioned me. "I find it hard to believe that after eight thousand years, you're only now finding a gateway."

"I've discovered many gateways in many of my lives," I assured him. "Though this is not a journey I intended to make without purpose."

"Finally come to kill me, have you?" Lucifer chuckled, sending a chill up my spine. "You truly believe you can take my life?"

"No, not necessarily. You will lift my curse, Devil, and I may reconsider."

"And why would I do that?"

"I'll kill you if you don't."

The moment the words left my mouth, Lucifer sprang forward, descending the steps of his throne in a single bound. He crashed down in front of me, his hand instantly gripped around my neck.

"You dare threaten me, Orm? After all I have given to you?" said Lucifer, examining me while I was in his hold. "What foolish errand have you allowed the mortals to send you on?"

"Not mortals," I struggled to say.

"Speak," demanded the Devil as he loosened his grip. "While I still allow you your life."

"Gods…" I told him. "Gods sent me."

Lucifer smashed his massive fist into my face, cracking my jaw and breaking my nose. The heat instantly flared up, beginning to repair the damage inflicted. "There are no other gods," he declared, tossing me into a column. My body smashed through it, stopped only by the wall behind it. I groaned as I collapsed to the floor. The room repaired itself quicker than I healed. "Only pretenders," Lucifer finished.

"Like you?" I said as I pushed myself onto my feet.

Lucifer rushed me, wrapping his hand around my neck again before I could stand. I gripped his arm with my hands as I called upon the heat. I buried my fingers into his flesh, my grip melting through to the bone. He cried out, releasing me as he stumbled back. The Devil clenched his arm as he turned back to me, charred holes dripping black blood from his body.

"You miserable creature!" he raged, lunging forward once again. I rolled aside as he flew past me. Lucifer bellowed, turning after me. I got on my feet before his next charge. "You'll die for your impudence, Orm!" he spat as he reached for me.

"No, not today, Lucifer." I brought up my hands, the heat within me burning perfectly. "Today, you die by the flame."

Fire leapt from my hands, washing over the Devil in a burning tidal wave. He cried out, falling back as I rose to my feet, still baptizing him in the flame. I let the flames feed off my rage, my agony. Eight thousand years of suffering washed over the Devil in perfect form, a fiery representation of all I had endured. In the end, I would be the one to kill Lucifer after all. It could be no one else. He created his own undoing, the very thing that would destroy him, by making me the first demon. I was Hell incarnate.

Lucifer screamed as my flames engulfed him. I dropped to my knees as the last of my power burned him down, exhausted from the feat. His screams quickly died, replaced by the crackling of the fire. I groaned as I collapsed. My strength was drained, leaving me crumpled on the marble floor. I needed some time to recover but that was fine. Nothing mattered anymore. I had finally killed the Devil.

The Shadow was right. I was the Champion of Hell. Only I alone stood a chance. I started to chuckle, laughing to myself softly as I thought about my eight-thousand-year-old curse. What if I had just come here in the beginning, after I found the first gateway? Could I have killed him then? There wasn't any point in thinking about it now. I couldn't go back in time and change the events of my life, and so I did what I always did. I moved on with a quick laugh of temporary insanity.

While I laughed, someone else began to laugh with me. My laughter quickly died then but the other person continued, laughing louder and louder. I felt it in my head and all around me, as if Hell itself was mocking me. I turned then as he emerged from the flames, unfazed by my fiery rage. "Why did you stop laughing, Orm?" Lucifer asked, stepping clear of the fire. "Thought you could kill me, did you? How amusing."

I shook my head and looked up at the ceiling, still too weak to stand. The ceiling was decorated with stories of the Devil from across time, all told in an elegant detailed hand with grace and passion. My eyes locked onto a mural of me, the day I became the first demon. I stared into the red eyes of hellhound Lucifer, the crimson color seeming to shine as the eyes looked back at me. I tried to push myself up but Lucifer kicked me back down. "Stay down, fool," he started. "You can't kill me, not as long as the curse remains. You exist to serve me. Or have you forgotten what you are?"

"Kill me," I pleaded. "Please end this."

"That sounds familiar," said Lucifer with a wicked smile, looking up at his storied past. "You've always been pathetic, Orm."

The Devil brought his fist down, slamming it into my gut and gripping my spine. I spat up blood as he hoisted me up and tossed me toward his throne. I crashed into the steps, taunted by the throne room repairing itself while I was too weak to heal. The fire inside me had just started to reignite itself but it was already flickering away as I felt myself dying. Lucifer walked over to me as I struggled to push myself up, slamming a foot down on the back of my head, crushing me into the floor. The heat flared more and more inside me, working desperately to keep me alive. "You're a monster," I barely managed to say.

Lucifer grabbed me by my neck and pulled me close so he could whisper in my ear. "So are you," he reminded me as he dropped me back down into the rubble as the floor repaired itself. I was trying to pull myself together, get on my feet. "Speak to me, servant," said Lucifer as he picked me up again and sat me down on the steps as I slowly healed. "Tell me more of these gods you speak of."

I coughed up blood, leaning against the stairs to steady myself before I said, "The Oracle and the Shadow. They are trying to maintain the balance by destroying you."

"I know of them," said Lucifer, mostly to himself. "What reason do these pretenders have to see my end?"

"You plan to destroy mankind—to destroy Earth. They've seen a terrible war that will be the end of all things. They claim the Heavens will have no part, and humanity is doomed to burn by your will."

"There will be no war. My goal has never been Earth, though perhaps it will burn. Allow me to share with you the truth while I allow you to heal," said Lucifer as he sat on his throne. "And perhaps by the end, we will reach a new deal."

ANTHONY

JOSEPH AND I SPRINTED ACROSS THE DESERT valley, rushing past collapsed structures as the wraiths screamed after us. Luka was nowhere to be found and, evidently, the wraiths were unbothered by sunlight. Without the Shadow to keep them at bay, the creatures stormed out of the temple and sprouted grotesque, leathery wings from their backs. They were chasing us on the ground and from the sky.

Joseph stumbled against me as we ducked into the ruins of a tower. I caught him before he fell, easing him against the wall. He forced his keys into my hand before letting go of me. The message was obvious.

"I'm not leaving you, man," I protested.

"You have to," he said through gritted teeth. He showed me his shoulder then, revealing a deep bloody gash from when the wraiths took him. I hadn't even noticed how bloodied he was until now.

"I'm not leaving you behind," I reassured him as the wraiths flew overhead. The Oracle had lied to us and it clearly didn't care for me, but its host had saved my life over and over again. I owed it to him to save him at least once.

"No one will be left behind." We looked into the far corner of the room as the shadows shifted. They formed into the figure of the cloaked man. "They're frenzied," said Luka plainly, emerging from the darkness. "They fear me on the surface and the demon below."

"Where have you been, Shadow?" Joseph demanded to know, though I assumed it was the Oracle. "Why did you leave us?"

"Save your strength, my friend," said Luka as he raised his hands. His shadows expanded, sealing us inside the ruins. We were safe, if only for a little while.

"Get the kid out of here," said Joseph. "He's mortal."

"He must stay," said Luka without acknowledging me. "When he returns, Lordal will need his vessel."

"You're certain he'll return?" said Joseph.

"Of course. Even if he dies, he'll return. It's his curse."

"You know what I mean. Did you tell him—"

"No," Luka cut him off. He turned to me as if he just remembered I was with them. I had felt so important before we got here, like I was becoming some powerful god. I felt meaningless without Lordal. The entities didn't even care to fill me in anymore. "You must be ready for Lordal's return, Anthony Monroe," Luka continued. "My power is strained maintaining your separation. I will unite you as soon as I feel the gateway open."

"I'll be ready," I assured him.

"Allow me to ease your pain," said Luka to Joseph, as if I was no longer in the room again. Shadows flowed like water spilling out of Luka's hand as he held it over Joseph's wound, filling it until it became a thick black scar. Joseph rotated his shoulder, impressed with the result, and got back on his feet. He thanked Luka and we stood in silence for a moment, listening to the wraiths surrounding us.

"So," Joseph started, "what's the plan?"

Before Luka could answer, a wraith smashed its head through the ceiling of the ruins, screeching as it tried to force its way through the barrier of shadows. Luka flicked a hand at it, decapitating the creature as the shadows closed around its neck. The creature's head landed with a loud thud and a mild splat, making me feel sick to my stomach.

"We need to get out of the Slats," said Luka. "How did you two get here?"

I jingled Joseph's keys in the air. "The Jeep is parked just outside of the valley," Joseph told Luka as they looked from the keys in my hand to each other. "But there are dozens of those wraiths to outrun. We won't make it."

"We have to try." Luka stroked his chin in thought. "We don't need to outrun them. I can kill a few, as can you."

"No," said Joseph. "I lost my backpack in the stairwell, and I'm still learning how to use my powers. My shotgun isn't killing any of those things. I'm just a regular guy, man."

I wondered what Joseph meant — what power he was talking about. I thought he could only see the future, and I knew he wasn't even really good at that yet.

"Doesn't matter," said Luka. "We need to—"

I suddenly cried out as the heat shot through my spine and extended through my body, forcing me to my knees. The pain dulled quickly as the heat left me, but my panic remained. Beads of sweat ran down my forehead as I looked around frantically.

Luka and Joseph knelt down by my side, both looking around as well. We all seemed to notice it at the same time. The wraiths had been silenced.

"What's going on?" said Joseph, reaching for his shotgun.

The valley grew quiet to the truth only I knew. The truth of what had just occurred. I spoke his name then, in the softest whisper. "Lordal," I said quietly. "He's returned."

Luka retracted his barrier then, allowing the shadows to return to his own. He paused, tilting his head with his eyes closed. "I cannot unite you two from such a distance," he told me. "We need to find him."

"Slowly," Joseph added. "I lost a lot of blood. I don't heal like a demon."

We made our way out of the ruins we hid in. I helped Joseph, offering him my shoulder for support as we walked out to the valley. I rested him against a fallen slab of stone before following Luka up to the top of a crumbled column for a better view. The straggling wraiths turned their attention back to us but Luka flicked his wrist, sending blades of shadows to cut them in half before they could alert the others, though it didn't matter.

An explosion sent a shockwave through the valley and we watched as the temple ahead of us burst into flames. The arches that formed the entryway exploded, releasing hellfire into the valley. Flames rose out from what remained, towers of fire that rose higher and higher, stretching skyward. Once they had reached above the temple, the flames separated into streaks of fire, each dancing across the sky in the various directions of the wraiths. The monsters seemed to sense the danger, screeching in fear as the flames surged towards them. The first of the wraiths touched by the hellfire burst into flames, burning as it fell to the Earth. It hit the ground, bursting into a cloud of gray ash, and we shielded our eyes against the ones that followed.

"What's happening?" I asked as the sky was illuminated by the spectacle unfolding above us. "What's going on?"

Luka shook his head and said, "I have no idea. We need to get back to Joseph."

We made our way back down the column, ducking as disintegrating wraiths fell past us. The valley was quickly turning gray, blanketed in the sudden ash.

"Something's wrong," Joseph whispered as we reached him, as he watched the sky. He muttered it three or four times, one hand holding his head as he did. The Oracle was speaking to him.

"What is it?" I asked. The wraiths' screams were quickly dying as the flames continued to rage after them. The few that managed to return to the temple were quickly destroyed, pursued by the flames back into the depths of the structure. When the last of the grotesque creatures had fallen, the flames returned, bringing themselves together before us. They began to weave together, slowly taking on the form of a familiar man. I never thought I'd be happy to see the demon again.

"Are you alright?" I asked, running to catch Lordal as he collapsed to the ground. He slammed a fist into the dirt to steady himself.

Lordal nodded slowly. "Yes," he said quietly.

"Then... It's over?" I asked, looking at the others. "We won?"

"No," said Lordal, louder now as he stood.

I looked back at him, panicked by his tone. "No?" I asked nervously.

"No." He shook his head slowly. "No, not all."

"Anthony, get away from him!" said Luka. He held his hands tense at his side, covering them in darkness. "He is no longer bound by my power."

Before I could move, Lordal snatched me off my feet with a hand around my throat. He grinned as he looked up at me, tightening his grip around my neck. I wrapped my hands around his wrist as I struggled to break free, but I knew it was no use. He no longer wore Luka's shackles on his wrists.

"Why?" was all I could manage to croak out as dots began to dance across my vision. "Why?"

"Put him down!" shouted Joseph. He was on his feet now, aiming his shotgun. "Put him down, Lordal! Or I swear to God I'll fire this shit straight through your fucking skull!"

"Don't play the hero now, Oracle," said Lordal, shaking his head. "You're the one that brought him here."

"Why are you doing this, Lordal?" Luka asked as he called the shadows towards him, preparing to face the demon. "We had a deal."

Lordal snorted at the remark. "I learned the truth, Shadow. So, I made a new deal — a better one — and it starts with me killing Anthony Monroe."

Lordal's grip tightened around my neck. "Orm…" I said with my last breath as my eyes began to well up with tears. "Please."

"How do you know my name?" Lordal asked, confused by his ancient title. He seemed shocked to find that someone knew his true name at all. Then, more angrily, he asked again. "How do you know my name, boy?"

"Oracle…" I gasped, just as I felt my lungs were ready to burst inside me. This would be my final breath.

His eyes narrowed, flames of anger raging in his pupils. Lordal tossed me aside into a nearby toppled column before I fell to the ground in pain. I gasped for air as he turned his sights to Joseph. I rubbed the flesh of my neck as Lordal stepped towards the Oracle, pointing a finger at the man.

"I tire of you and your games, Oracle," he growled. "If you value your life, stay out of my way, Joseph St. Claire."

"Lordal, don't do this," said Joseph, lowering his shotgun. "This is bigger than you. You know that. Lucifer is using you, just like he always has. It's what he does."

"Don't bother with him, Joseph." Luka stepped forward. "He's always been the Devil's dog. He always will be."

"Silence!" Lordal roared at them. "I don't care about either of your lies anymore. At least tell the boy the truth before I end his life. Tell him about the book, about what you really are. You just needed to get me here, and the boy? Nothing but a vessel. You knew he'd never leave this desert. You brought him here to die."

My heart shattered as I realized how meaningless I truly was to these entities. I couldn't believe it was Lordal who was angry about how I was treated, though I understood it was only because he was betrayed too.

Joseph lowered his head. The all-knowing Oracle had nothing to say. Luka stepped forward but it was too late. Lordal raised a hand and a wall of flames rose from the ground, separating us from them. He turned to face me, the wall of fire illuminating his massive figure. On the other side, I could just see Luka struggling beyond the flames, looking for some way to reach me. It was no use though.

The world's first demon loomed over me; emotion absent from his eyes. His face remained expressionless. There was no joy in what he was doing, or sadness, or even anger. It was then that I realized I was truly nothing to him. I was just the latest in a long line of hosts and now he had decided he was done with me. I began struggling to my feet, never breaking eye contact with him.

"So, you're really going to do this?" I asked him. I used what remained of the column I slammed through to steady myself as I got on my feet. I leaned against the rubble, exhausted but not afraid. I would face my demon. "You're really going to kill me, Lordal?"

He didn't answer immediately. He just stood there, staring at me as I stared at him. The crackling of the fire muffled the shouts of Luka and Joseph on the other side. I could see shadows trying to breach the flames, but to no avail. Eventually, I couldn't stand it anymore — waiting to die.

"Just do it already," I shouted, lunging forward.

My eyes widened as I was caught midair, his hand once again around my throat. His grip tightened slowly as Lordal said his final words to me.

"I am sorry, Anthony Monroe."

Then my neck snapped with a loud crack that echoed through my body, and my life faded out.

EPILOGUE

I WATCHED FROM THE RIDGE OF THE VALLEY AS the demon took another innocent life. The two men on the other side of the flames cried out but he had no interest in them. He called upon the flame, allowing it to envelop him and the body he carried in a swirling heap of fire. The flames flickered away until there was nothing but embers and scorch marks where he had stood. There was no knowing where he had gone, but I would find him again. I always did.

I reached into my jacket pocket, pulling out a local newspaper. It was written in Spanish but I had learned the language a long time ago. The front-page story was **Hell on Earth: Burned Remains Discovered, Old City District Destroyed**. What a fitting title. Hell on Earth. I stuffed the newspaper back into my pocket. Retrieving my sword and pack from the dirt, I got on my feet and started my way down into the valley, to the strange men Lordal left behind.

ABOUT THE AUTHOR

Stephan Augustine currently resides in the San Francisco Bay Area. He enjoys traveling to new and exciting places while he works. Most days, he can be found scribbling into notebooks and pinning pages onto bulletin boards, all in an effort to complete his next entry in his multiverse-spanning series.

Stephan is passionate about his stories, working to create a dark and expansive reality for his audience to lose themselves within. In it, he intends to explore the vast depths and possibilities of fantasy and science fiction, weaving together an astonishing saga, tapestried from many unique and diverse tales.

Connect with him on Instagram (@stephan.augustine)

Made in the USA
Columbia, SC
10 December 2023

760caa2e-0fc7-44be-953b-62e67dcd69fbR01